Thank you, Ojou-san and Holly, for encouraging me to turn my childhood dream of writing into reality.

Solomon Li

OSAKA SUNSET

AUSTIN MACAULEY PUBLISHERS™

LONDON • CAMBRIDGE • NEW YORK • SHARJAH

ISBN – 9789948356325 – (Paperback)
ISBN – 9789948356318 – (E-Book)

Application Number: MC-10-01-6082694
Age Classification: 17+

The age group that matches the content of the books has been classified according to the age classification system issued by the National Media Council.

First Published (2020)
AUSTIN MACAULEY PUBLISHERS FZE
Sharjah Publishing City
P.O Box [519201]
Sharjah, UAE
www.austinmacauley.ae
+971 655 95 202

A heartfelt 'Arigatou' to Japan for the wonderful experience. Special mentions to Jakov for getting me out of my comfort zone, Oscar for being my personal taxi and to 'Paris/Calvin' for their help in Osaka.

Disclaimer: Any resemblance to real-life persons or events is coincidental. The author maintains that this is just a story despite drawing from real-world inspirations.

A man whose family is urging him to marry decides that before his next birthday, he would try to resolve his romantic lingerings. He is not sure whether or not he wants to marry the bride chosen for him, or if he will devote himself to a celibate priesthood. Needing to explore how he feels completely, he goes to Japan to consult with his best friend, and after some reflection, steels himself for what awaits in Osaka. He is going to meet with the girl who captured his heart all those years ago, and hopefully come to a conclusion about love and life.

Chapter 1

My phone alerts me to a new message. A Tinder message. Selfie too. Not a new match, but a new message from the girl last week. I quickly glance, out of habit more than interest. Dating was not something I wanted to think about right now, not ever since dinner with my parents last week. I think back to that conversation, the surprise and the silent sense of alarm it gave me. If I'm being honest, still gives me. Seeing that I was lost in my own ambivalence, Oscar looks over from his mobile game. 'Stick Wars', now with 'Unlimited Zombies Mode'. We both tried it out a month ago, and it wasn't a surprise to see that Oscar was addicted to the gameplay. In a different time, he would have made a fearsome battle commander. As he was born at the end of the 20th century, he had to settle for studying politics and military history: he stayed informed about global situations, especially the more explosively charged ones. Has a pretty keen mind for intel too, although at this moment he was using those analytical skills to strategically determine how much clothing my Tinder girl wasn't wearing.

"She's cute. And if I'm reading this right, she's definitely wild in the sack – you hooked up with her yet?" Oscar's steady tone is always to point, and not in a bad way: he doesn't believe in pretence or playing 'pointless games'. We often debate the significance of 'the social dance', and try as I might to convince him otherwise, he is a man true to his nature, which is very straightforward. Though some of his ex-girlfriends have expressed annoyance with it (and some being driven to the brink of despair!). I wouldn't have it any other way though. A man who is true to himself is someone you can make accurate assessments with, and ever since my best friend, Vik, moved away, I have come to rely on Oscar's strangely blunt finesse.

"Hmmm, I've met her! She's very interesting, planning on doing her masters in nano-organic robotics, or something like that. But no, nothing too intimate yet – I'll just play it cool for now."

The truth was, while this girl and I did have some very deep conversations, when we met up, something was missing. A spark of some sort. As usual. It wasn't for lack of physical temptation either. Jennifer, or Jiggy as she liked to be called, had short-ish red hair that was still long enough to be tied back when need arose, a pretty face framed by a fringe that suggested a carefree spirit and emerald green eyes that suggested mischief. Her slim figure still had plenty of curves in all the right places (which would have been a crime to neglect mentioning), garnished by tattoos that only seemed to enhance her passion for robotics. Her appeal was high, on paper anyway. Oscar finishes his 'tactical reconnaissance' and returns to defending against an endless horde of the undead. Casually, almost too casually, he asks me,

"So, Thomas, I'm guessing this isn't the one either?"

Silence fills the room, punctuated rather than disturbed by the occasional clicks coming from his mobile game. Though we do not speak, the silence is a comfortable one between us. These days it is not uncommon for us to spend maybe 30–40 minutes at a time immersed in our own phones, before resuming our conversations. I normally contrast with him, being a man of words and wit and prose, but now I was stricken dumbfound. As usual, Oscar hits the nail on the head. So I begin to relate the pseudo-ultimatum my parents and I held over dinner last week.

We met for dinner at Father's restaurant. He was the Head Chef and normally worked until late night, but I figured that he was probably taking his dinner break with us. I have to admit that I was nervous, as my parents don't normally meet, not since they separated last year. I felt a

trace amount of dread at the news being health related. Yet a part of me was relieved to see them. Maybe I was just happy that they were being civil in public, less bickering and angry looks at one another, or worse. Father was a man of few words, but Mother could talk from sunrise until sunset. She is clearly where I get my talkative genes. However, I immediately sensed something was off once they begun mentioning how old I was getting. Mother directs the conversation,

"My dearest son, you are turning 29 in a few weeks. At this point, it's time to start thinking about settling down. Your father and I want to know, do you have anyone special in your life?"

I did not answer immediately. But to continue my silence would be very unfilial of me.

"I do not currently have a girlfriend."

"Well, it just so happens that a friend of mine saw a picture of you, and she recommended her niece to me. I saw a photo and spoke to her over the phone. She's younger by about 4 years, but very mature, and a lovely temperament. We think she will make a proper match for you, my handsome, clever boy! What do you say?"

I admit, despite my calm mask, a shock went through my body. Marriage? And an arranged one at that! I try to gather my thoughts, as I joke nervously.

"Mother, do you owe these people money or something? Am I to be sold off to pay a debt? If that's the issue, then tell me! We can work out a payment plan, right? Hahah!"

At this point my father clears his throat, sobering my attitude. Father has a husky voice from smoking so much, brimming with authority, one I recall from childhood as stern yet not unkind.

"Son, you are nearly thirty, and we haven't seen you with a steady partner since you were 20. I don't completely agree with your mother's method, but I do wish to see you married and finally have children."

"But you and Mother already have grandchildren! Big sister has given you two lovely granddaughters, who visit all the time too. So why are we discussing this?"

My mother interjects, "My eldest son, I have loved you the most of all my children, though a mother should not ought to have favourites. From the moment you were born, I knew you would be special! It would give us great joy to see you married at last with the right girl. And believe me when I say that if I didn't think this girl was good enough for you, I wouldn't recommend her. In fact, I have been arranging with my friend, who lives in Germany, to bring her and her family here to meet with you! They'll arrive in about a month. Officially it's to see their extended family, but her mother seems very keen on this idea. Couldn't you meet with them and give her a chance?"

Again, I am silent as I consider the options. I could not explain everything to my parents, about why I had not had a steady partner in almost a decade. But that is a conversation no child wants to have with their parents. So instead, I level with them by announcing something that I had entertained years ago and had seriously considered for the last 6 months.

"Actually, Father, Mother, I do not know how to tell you this… but I am making plans to join a priesthood. To become a practicing ascetic. I want to focus on spirituality and enlightenment over marriage and children. Please do not think your son ungrateful, it is simply a calling that I do not believe right to ignore. Naturally, a marriage is out of the question along this path."

At this point, I felt a twinge of guilt as my mother's enthusiasm visibly diminished. There was truth in this though; as a child I would often spend time with my maternal grandfather in the makeshift temple Father constructed in the backyard. Complete with altar, kneeling cushions and a seemingly endless supply of candles and incense. I learned of Buddhist mantras, abstained from meat long after he passed away and regularly studied scriptures of different religions as the years went by. Happy, simple times, for I was a boy drawn to the idea of deities and the endless pursuit of self-cultivation. Even after I hit puberty, and discovered girls (as well as fried chicken), I've always been deeply interested in spirituality and philosophy. Owing to a lack of romantic connection with females, I had been considering just throwing in the towel, and devoting myself to a less complicated pathway.

Father recovered first. "Well, there is a certain nobility in that, though I am very sorry to hear it. Your children would have been born with my family name, but I think our ancestors would understand. Still, you sound as if you have doubts. Very well, I propose this: if you still feel this way after you turn 29, we will support you in your calling and thank the heavens you have brothers. But if you are not prepared to commit by then, you will meet with this girl, and if she is acceptable, we will start planning your betrothal. Is that understood?"

My father was never a man to mince words, and by his solid, defined tones I understood the message clearly. If I could not get on with my life, my parents would 'help' me do so. This conversation was over, for now at least. I had bought myself two weeks of time, but after that, who knew what my future held?

"Sweet Jesus!" I initially think Oscar has verbally recoiled from the revelation, but no, it is just him trying to stand. His knee is acting up again. This man is a man's man, born to fight, which he did regularly at mixed martial arts training or amateur competitions. We're all waiting for the day he makes it to the professional league; there'll be waves, guaranteed. If his body holds out first.

"Don't scare me like that! You know how much effort I put into your recovery. Nursing you back to 'health' isn't easy you know." I smile, as Oscar merely shrugs off my concern.

"If you could maybe take a look at the knee again before I go, that'd be good? So, your parents are saying get married or stop having fun. Hmm, basically just stop having fun… Is your bride hot at least? If so, it sounds better than not having sex again."

"Hah! I don't know what she looks like, but my mum insists she's very pretty. Maybe you should consider the priesthood too, we could make exemplary holy men!"

"You know, I have thought about it, or something similar, like joining the military long term. Life's less complicated without women and children I suppose."

"There is no life without women, my friend, isn't that what you've always told me? You just have to learn to live with them!" I am feeling almost normal as my mocking/teasing banter continues. Oscar gets back to the point.

"So, what are you going to do?"

I sigh and shrug. He sits back down and I start to inspect Oscar's knee. The ligaments are not in great shape, while the kneecap is looser than ideal for a human, but after some kneading the inner tension is massaged along, and his limb visibly relaxes. I do take some pride in my massage skills, something that's always been a big hit with the ladies. As part of my exploration into the spiritual nature of the world, I became very interested with internal energy theory and had taken a course in Chinese pressure point massage therapy. It usually takes months or even years to build up the required hand strength, at least if you don't want them cramping within five minutes. Didn't finish it, but I daresay I left with some very strong fingers.

"How does that feel, Oscar? Any stiffness?"

"Better. Definitely less painful. Could we speed up the process? I have another fight next month."

"… Your body isn't made to take such punishment. I'm surprised you're not getting off on the pain somehow! Maybe you should focus on more flexibility exercises."

"Okay, thanks. I should probably get going now."

Oscar had come by for dinner, and it was nearly 10 pm now. I accompany him outside, where we take a moment to gaze at the night sky. The evening air is cool, something which helps clear my thoughts a little. I wish him a safe ride home as he drives away and make my way back inside. It all boils down to marriage or celibacy: I'm torn between a sense of filial duty, and enlightenment (or at the very least, the pursuit of it). Maybe this situation is typical of someone seeking spiritualism, yet simultaneously using dating apps? Pacing around my home, I notice that further musings have not gained me any new insights and instead lost me two hours. I need to be somewhere early-ish tomorrow, so I decide to go to bed. As a great philosopher once said, "F*ck it!" Okay, I'm paraphrasing, but I'm also fairly certain that all philosophers have said something along those lines, at least once in their lives.

Chapter 2

The seminar room is reasonably packed, a testament to the time-tested appeal of 'refreshments provided'. I pause, swallowing to alleviate my dry mouth. A combination of jitters and 10 minutes of talking. The audience is comprised mostly of older citizens, with a sparse patch of the typical hippy crowd, and the occasional suit, likely business folk seeking something to use at their annual workplace retreats. I continue where I left off,

"Let us break down the word 'defile'. Just saying it induces a strong imagery. One of something being violated, molested even, and hence, for that reason alone it is considered wrong. Vile. Evil. *Defile.* We all think we know what it means, to taint, to somehow diminish the purity of something. Yet, I ask you, ladies and gentlemen, what do we get when we want the opposite? If something dehumanises you, you are no longer human? So if I don't want it defiled, then I suppose I could say I want it filed? And the word *file* now has a different connotation, one of neatness and order. Thus, by that reasoning, to defile is inherently bad because it doesn't fit into what structured society considers to be correct! Now, once we see it in this light, we might feel sorry for the word, mightn't we? After all, it's not the word's fault that our human minds are prone to seeking rationale and patterns. It makes sense because it makes sense? How paradoxical does that sound! For this reason we must ask ourselves, what is the nature of the world? Is it order, or chaos, or a mix of both? This is what led to the first Gothic literature, the premise that our neat and ordered lives are actually unnaturally so, and behind the veneer of politeness and rules, there is a maelstrom of chaos waiting to erupt. So we get a sort of social hypocrisy, a façade. Now, rather than draw attention to the Victorians (*several chuckles reverberate throughout the audience*), I want us to focus on an ideology where chaos is considered natural, and order, at least how humans see it, is unnatural. I am talking about Taoism, specifically the concept of Wu Wei. It's often translated as meaning 'no action'; it is actually closer to considering it a form of 'non-interference'. Imagine living life without having to micromanage! Think about it... and then realise that by thinking about it, you've lost it (*more chuckles litter the crowd*). However, by not thinking about it, you will have retained it. That specific conclusion, ladies and gentlemen, is the state of mind that we often referred to as Zen, and I hope you all find yours. Remember, it'll be in the places you don't look for it – thank you very much!"

The audience claps and I take a bow. As I return to my seat on the panel, with the other guest speakers, the host takes my place at the lectern.

"And that was our last guest speaker, Mr Thomas Kei on finding your Zen. Another round of applause!"

The audience complies, though they are a patchwork of enthusiasm. Sitting for two hours through seven guest speakers' talk about 'Mindfulness' was ironically dull, though I suppose most people will only be here if they wanted to be. Still, it was exciting enough for me, if only because I was not a regular at these affairs. I normally get invited to a handful every month, but being asked to present was rare, so naturally I was keen to engage the audience.

"As with the other guest speakers, Mr Kei will now answer some questions. Yes?" A few hands go up, it seems that there was no need for plants. Although it seems a shady practice, there are club members planted in the audience, and their use was quite ethical. Often, they would just reiterate key points for the audience's benefit, or save a guest speaker from the embarrassment of an uninterested crowd – some topics are terribly esoteric. I sip on some water, to rehydrate my mouth after the 15 minutes spent orating, as I wait. An older man, slightly overweight, with thin spectacles that framed light eyes addresses me.

"Mr Kei–"

"Please, just 'Tom' will do, 'Mr Kei' makes me feel so old!" as I interject, I smile broadly, as a means to encourage the audience, maybe even build a rapport.

The man is visibly more relaxed as he continues, "Very well, Tom, (*chuckles litter the room*) – as I was saying, I noticed that your speech contained a lot of elements touching on tangential comprehension. I just want to know, was this deliberately done, so as to deconstruct the notion of learning as linear?" I am impressed by this obvious academic, not everyone can easily follow my speech structure. It's actually less to do with bamboozling my audience, and more to do with layering my points. I take a moment to compose myself, before answering,

"There's a lot I want to discuss about your point, but time is pressing so I will try to be brief. I'm glad you noticed the structure of my oration, and yes, the structure is deliberate. There's a concept I always use to explain the limitations of linear thinking, which often stumps conventionally clever folks who unfortunately lack mental diversity. Such people, for all their intelligence, can have their thought processes reduced to a straight line, but could you imagine trying to understand a circle with just straight lines? The mathematical expression of tangents is what I use to highlight this thinking process. A lot of metaphysics needs one to accept that not everyone can imagine a circle, especially when they are used to thinking in straight lines. Phew, that was a mouthful! I hope I answered your question?" The gentleman nods repeatedly, and I daresay even approvingly, before sitting back down.

Another question is raised, this time from a young brunette girl in her early 20s.

"Could you clear something up for me? You mentioned before that to defile is probably considered evil because humans like things to be neat and orderly, yet is it natural then for depravity and lawlessness to run rampant? I'm not saying you condone it, but how can rape and sexual violence be considered natural, especially when we're discussing mindfulness?"

This question manages to rouse the interest of the crowd. Maybe this woman is trying to off balance me, or maybe she is genuinely curious. I wasn't worried.

"Firstly, let me thank you for not accusing me of condoning rape. For the record, I don't. But to the point, let me see if I understand your question. I used the term 'defile' only to demonstrate a point, that humans like things to be organised to varying degrees. However, when used in the way you've applied, the act of defiling is about sexual and material exploitation. Which did, does and unfortunately probably will continue. Is it something instinctual, like several social psychologists have postulated? Is it a question of violence, or sex? Let us ask ourselves, is sex natural? Of course it is, otherwise we wouldn't be here! (*I draw encouragement from the tittering of the audience members.*) In the past, there were double standards abound for men and women concerning sexual etiquette, and the restrictions imposed were supposedly to protect women, or control them, for the more cynical minded. Rather than prohibit it, classic Taoism encouraged sexual freedom, if only because they didn't overthink it like most polite societies would. It might surprise you that the earliest Taoist texts on spirituality had a section which could give the Karma Sutra a run for its money! But back to the topic, a woman who had been defiled *sexually* was often so because she had sex in a way that *her society* didn't permit. And that is the crux of it all, for society is ultimately a structure designed to be orderly and ordered, whereas true Zen doesn't need to try to be ordered. It just happens to be at times. If you are looking at it from a certain angle. That is true mindfulness, being aware naturally without doing so forcibly."

She continues her line of questioning, "Does that mean we should just accept things the way they are, without introspecting how we feel about it?"

"Reflection is essentially introspection, just less judgmental! I'm grateful you asked this, as I didn't cover much on Wu Wei specifically today. It does not mean giving up control, rather it is understanding that no one has complete control, and going along with the unimpeded flow is the best way to get to where you are. Naturally, if you are on fire, you put out the flames, but you can imagine how clumsy it would be to panic and over-think each step. Someone who understands acceptance would simply put out the flames the best way they could. Stop, drop, and roll, or jump into a water body. Does that answer your question? If not, I'll be delighted to speak to you in person afterwards." I give a smile, which I was glad to see returned, and continue with a few more questions from a few more people, though none as loaded as hers.

After the Q and A, the host thanks everyone, and we make our way out. I see the same brunette in the parking lot outside. Mildly unexpected but not unwelcome company. Up close, I see that she has an intelligent questioning gaze, and sharp features, but her smile softens the latter. She just looks at me, so I respond first.

"Hello. I take it that I failed to satisfy your curiosity back there?"

"Actually, I'm just waiting for my ride. You were really good up there, almost like you were doing stand-up instead of an academic lecture! Especially at the end. Sorry if I was rude, I sort of enjoy putting deep thinkers on the spot, they usually don't respond well to spontaneity."

"Oh, is that the impression you got? Forgive me for misleading you, I'm not a deep thinker in the slightest! Probably why I wasn't fazed." She smiles, amused perhaps by my playful tones, or perhaps just being polite. It was hard to get a read on this girl, her demeanour switched from aloof to curious every few seconds.

"Well, it was fun to see a philosopher type being fun to listen to. You must be the youngest one up there?"

"Actually, the 3rd speaker was younger than me, he's 27. I'm 28, turning 29 pretty soon. I can understand why you'd think he's older though, I still have hair on my head, though not my face!"

We laugh at this, but to be honest, I have secretly always wanted to grow a beard. Oscar tells me that I'm lucky, it's an annoying maintenance and itchy too. I decide to open myself up a little to this curious girl.

"Actually, I felt that I could have done better. I was up late last night and after the rush of giving the speech, I'm sort of feeling it. I realise that being tired for a mindfulness speech is kinda ironic, but overall, thanks for liking it."

"It's cool. Did you drive? You should probably grab a coffee. You don't wanna crash in your car after all."

"Hah! Do you mean fall asleep or cause an accident?"

"Yes." She laughs, a light laughter that reminds me of wind chimes. Subtly but unmistakably teasing wind chimes. Then she smirks, the little minx. Clearly a person who likes power plays. That is fine, I can play along.

"So, you probably saved my life. I insist on repaying you! Maybe with a cup of lifesaving coffee? You may need more than one though. I'm not an interesting conversationalist."

"Sure, though, I'll be the judge of that. I know a great place farther down the street. Best lattes this part of the city."

"Really? I'll hold you to that. Um wait, what about your ride?"

"You are my ride, silly." Wow. This girl really knows what she wants and isn't shy about getting it. Or she's a subtle bitch. I guess I'll find out soon enough.

We make general conversation until we get to the location. Barely five minutes. After I park, we make our way to the café that supposedly boasts the best lattes around. I've actually done a barista's introductory course with Oscar, even though I usually prefer teas. Clueless as I was, Pierre, the instructor, was very patient and clearly an artisan of his craft. He was French, thus both romantic and realistic in his expectations. For instance, he warned us that most Italian coffee connoisseurs would be snobs, but he also reminded everybody that good coffee was an expression of the heart, and ugly hearts would ruin otherwise beautiful coffee. Monsieur Pierre St Claire was able to impart his respect for coffee on to myself, admittedly an elitist when it came to teas. I recall what I had learned that sunny afternoon in his studio, and begin to make assessments unto this cafe. At first, I'm not impressed, as there are open and exposed glass canisters. Filled with Robusta beans, which is famous for bitter black coffee, though I can distinguish the occasional Arabica bean mixed in. Pierre has taught us that fresh beans are essential, and while he doesn't shun Robusta, Arabica beans are superior by far. This entire place seems a little hipster to me, a mix of post-postmodern with just enough sensibility to be considered artistic, yet it does seem to be tailored for this girl's personality. Speaking of which, "Hey, this is kind of weird, but who do I have the pleasure of sitting with? I just realised I never asked your name!"

"Took you long enough. It's Becky. And I forgive you!" She gives a short laugh, which underlines the regal, almost challenging attitude she presents to the world. It's cute, especially as her petite figure gave the impression of a much more subdued personality. We order the lattes, and as I observe the barista's work, I soften my initial impression. The beans on display were only for display, thankfully, and the beans used in the espresso machines are a light brown, not covered by shiny film (a tell-tale sign of older beans). More importantly, the staff all adhere to good hygiene practices and didn't leave wiping cloths on random parts of the workstation. Pierre would be pleased.

I relate this to Becky, who nods with mild curiosity, and replies, "I just like the taste here. You know, like you said in the seminar, don't overthink, otherwise you'll lose the rhythm?"

"You have a good memory. What made you come to the seminar in the first place? You seem very clever, but not the type to look for inner peace, which is 90% of the usual crowd."

"You're right, I am very clever! It was the part about Zen actually. I've always been into Japanese culture, you know, anime, J-pop and food, of course! After finishing my degree in Japanese, I even lived in Japan for a year – teaching English to middle school kids."

Upon hearing this, I immediately feel a sense of danger, the kind that prey animals develop when specific predators may be about. But this is ridiculous! She was half my size and I certainly didn't feel inferior to her, intellectually speaking. I realise, however, that out of all the guest speakers, I was the only one who was Asian. Still, I maintain my poker face.

"That sounds amazing. My best friend moved to Japan last month with his girlfriend. They are having a great time while adjusting, apparently it's very different to the West over there?"

"Oh yeah, it's completely different, but I loved it! Speaking of which, where are you from, if you don't mind my asking? I know you're Asian but I can't seem to place exactly where, and it's bothering me."

"Hah, you wouldn't be the first. No, I'm a locally grown Asian, so it can be hard to tell. I think I have a trace amount of Japanese on my father's side, but it's not worth mentioning. I'm mainly Chinese, though if you have to include my nationalistic leanings, I would be Pro-British as well. Long Live the Imperial Monarchy! That being said… *Hajime mashite Becky-san, yoroshiku onegaishimasu.*"

Her eyes light up as I switch to Japanese, and she responds in turn.

"*Sugoi, nihon-go ga wakarimasu ka*?! (Awesome, you understand Japanese?)" Her enthusiasm is curbed somewhat when I shake my head.

"No, but I am also immensely fond of the culture. Plus, my best friend and I have a bet going on that when he returns from Japan in two years, we would try to speak the language together. I'm learning a little bit at a time, mostly words and phrases, the occasional grammar video. His girlfriend doesn't speak much, but she works at an international school so she only needs to use English anyway."

"Oh yeah, but that's still pretty cool. I miss speaking Japanese on a daily basis, but I binge-watch their shows all the time so I hear it often enough. My boyfriend isn't that interested in the language, so it's a bit of a drag. He loves the culture, that's something." I take a moment to process this.

"You have a boyfriend? I mean, that's fine, but I kinda thought we were flirting here…?"

At this point, she looks over to me seriously, and I see that her eyes are actually looking directly into mine. A scan attack? I don't look away, but lean closer, meeting her gaze. We break away from our psychic battle, the tension dissipating slowly, as she responds, "We are. It's harmless fun, in my opinion at least. But when I saw you, I sort of got the impression that you weren't available? Almost as if you enjoy the hunt but you don't take any trophies. Like, looking at it more carefully now I don't think you have a girlfriend, and you're most likely straight, considering all the times you were stealing glances at my boobs." It is true that Becky does have a very full cleavage (for her size) but I'm playfully indignant all the same.

"I did no such thing! And even if I did, you're clearly the type of person who likes the attention. I would go so far as to say, a borderline exhibitionist?"

"You see? You're deflecting and getting defensive! So you must be hiding something. I'm pretty good at this you know." She starts laughing, and I join in. It was hard not to, considering we had just met, yet openly started profiling each other. As the mirth fizzles, she looks at me more seriously again.

"Well, is it true? Do you have someone? Or maybe, someone has you?"

I look away at this point, for this random girl is close to something I have tried to seal away for the last six years. But considering everything that is happening in my life, especially what had to happen soon, I decide to respond frankly.

"You are indeed perceptive. But it's not easy to talk about this, especially as I'm trying to forget. I did meet someone, a long time ago, and even though we didn't date, she had a big impact on my life. But lately, I feel like I just want to stop trying to find romance, and settle into a peaceful spiritual lifestyle, as a priest or something. Or a monk, though I like having hair, worldly possessions not withstanding. Does this make any sense to you?"

She takes a moment to consider what I've told her and wrinkles her nose as if to visibly indicate mental processing. "Erm, I think so. Basically, you're hung up on this one girl, and she was so amazing that you don't think anyone else is good enough for you, so you think running away is the answer. That's it, right?" Ouch, this girl can cut with her words! But her dissection is shallow, and she can only distinguish the form of my problem, not the essence.

"It's not that no one else is good enough. I do meet lots of girls. Really now, lower your eyebrows, young lady! But each time, I don't feel the same spark, or connection, you know? I thought after she left, I would get over her, but…"

"But you haven't. So… you're just running away from how you feel. Where did she go anyway?"

"She became a lawyer, works in Japan now. Um, she's part Japanese too so I guess it's not surprising."

"O-M-G, she's Japanese? Why didn't you say so!? Of course, in that case you can't give up on her!"

"Really? You can't be serious." I stare in mild shock. Becky tilts her head and squints at me for a second, before going back to normal.

"No, I'm just messing with you. Though she does sound pretty cool. Especially, if you've been into her all this time, when she isn't even around."

"Yeah, she was… beautiful, in every sense of the word." And I mean that. I recall a saying that when a man calls a woman pretty, he means her face; when he calls her hot, he means her body; when he says she's beautiful, he means her soul. Its prose is punctured somewhat by the assertion that regardless of any compliment, he still just wants to sleep with her.

"Did you get plastic surgery or something?"

"What?" I'm thrown off course by the question, not knowing what she means. Plastic surgery, is this some new age hipster slang?

"Well, you seem smart, and you dress pretty slick." I'm wearing an all-black outfit comprised of trousers, a short-sleeved black silk shirt tucked in and my favourite black blazer. What did this have to do with anything my face seemed to convey? She continued.

"You also seem fit, broad shoulders, and I find your personality quirky, but charming. So I figured that maybe you had plastic surgery since you've met her, coz I think you're okay looking. Not as handsome as my boyfriend, but nothing to hide up in a tower."

"Thank you, I do think that I am a notch above Quasimodo!" We laugh. I am flattered. Despite what my mother says, I do not consider myself good looking. Passable most days, but nothing special. I am told I have deeply soulful eyes and delicate cheekbones, plus in the right light, I have a nice smile, but photos are very hit and miss for me. Not that it should matter, as an enlightened individual should care less about physical appearance and more about the reflection of their soul. Something that Becky agrees with, but also mentions how it was different for girls, which I concede. I'm not an impractical spiritualist after all. I eventually answer her question.

"No surgery, I swear. Though I have cleaned up my look since I first met her. She made me more self-conscious of my appearance, so if you like what you see then it's partially thanks to her. I was a mess the first time I met her too, wild greasy hair, shabby clothes and I was sun burnt with blood-shot eyes from my summer job in the countryside. Women find that hot, right?"

"Wow, no wonder she left!" She laughs again, though I do not think unkindly. "It's good then, she left a positive impact on you. So, do you still talk to her, or were you more of the stalker type? I have been getting trace amounts of creepy vibes from you."

"Hey, don't joke about that! It hits too close to home." Despite my seemingly wounded tones, I smile to indicate that I was only teasing. "Every now and then. I haven't for a while, but I think she's doing okay, even though she works heaps. We hung out quite a bit, with mutual friends mostly, but by the time I wanted to tell her how I felt, she got an offer that she couldn't pass up. I don't blame anyone, but I always regretted not saying it to her face."

My teasing demeanour fades away as I recall that time six years ago when I found out she was leaving for good.

We were all at a group party, an end-of-year celebration for post exams. A few of our friends were already slightly buzzed from drinks, but mostly the atmosphere was one of relief. Another semester down, and we were all happy to express our gratitude for the upcoming holiday break. We were a mixed group, some having graduated, some still studying, and some who didn't really have any academic reason to stick around, but did it for the social ties. As the general chatter broke off into separate circles, hers was discussing holiday plans. She was talking to her best friends, Louise and Toby.

"Wow, you're going to Japan! That's awesome, when do you get back?"

"Well... I'm seeing my family there, but I got offered a job working in Osaka, and I think I'm definitely going to take it."

"What? You're leaving me??? You can't leave me! I thought we were study buddies!"

"We are, Louise, we'll always be! But this is something I've always wanted to do, in a city I've always wanted to live in. We'll keep in touch, and you have to visit me if you go there, okay?!"

"I still can't believe you're going, I'm going to miss you so much!!!"

"I'm going to miss you all too!"

I tune out of the conversation as I try to process everything. Later, as everything settles, some people leave, others stay behind, and I find a chance to sit next to her, just the two of us.

"Hey, you look sleepy! Time to go home?"

"Hey, Tom! Nah, I'm okay, it's just been a big day. Did you hear? I'm going to be working in Japan soon!"

"I did! And congratulations! It must be very exciting, but maybe a little daunting too?"

"A little, this is a new chapter of my life after all. But I've been there, and I love Japan! So yeah, it's all good."

"When do you leave? You're seeing family there too right?"

"Yeah, can't wait to see my mother again, and my cute little brother! I always like to remind him that I'm his big sister, even though he's taller than me now. I'm flying out in two days."

"Two days... that's so soon! You'll have a lot of friends who'll miss you. Maybe we can visit you, once you get settled in?"

"Sure! I'll take you all around town, show you the sights. And the restaurants too, all the food is really nice!"

"Uh oh, maybe we won't recognise you by then."

"Huh, why?"

"Because you'll be rounder! Hahah!" She laughs and shoves me playfully.

"Hah, you're so weird, Tom!"

"Yeah, but I wouldn't be me if I wasn't... hey, I'll miss you, Naomi."

"Aww, thank you! Oh, I have to go, my group is heading back to our apartment. Bye!" She gives me a quick hug, and I watch her leave through the doors. And although I didn't think of it at the time, out of my life.

I remained seated as time slowed to a standstill. Under my breath, to no one in particular, I whisper, "Goodbye."

"Um, is there a bug in your coffee?" Becky is watching me curiously as I reminisce.

"No, no… this conversation is just making me think about stuff I haven't in forever."

"Hmmm, can I ask you something, Thomas?" I indicate my willingness, and she continues, "When was your last serious relationship? Or even, when was the last time you had any kind of sex? Like, anything."

"That's kind of personal, don't you think?"

"Hey, I thought you said sex was natural!"

"Sex IS natural, but that doesn't mean I bring it up everywhere. Besides, our society is over-saturated with sexual obsession, and there are certain pursuits which are more fulfilling. I'm more interested in those. How come no one asks each other when their last epiphany was? Epiphanies are essentially spiritual orgasms you know." I am back to my mocking, playful self. Becky looks intrigued.

"Hmm, I'll have to look into that then." She's clearly not shy about her own sexuality. "But that's not what I was getting at. When was the last time you had intimate relations with a woman? Not even sex, just something meaningful."

The question stumps me. I have a habit of briefly entertaining the idea of dating, and I do meet several potential lovers each season. But I have never once made it to the point when it could be considered dating or romantically intimate. Deep conversations with my most recent girl were mostly about the nature of artificial simulations versus reality. Not on a relationship, though I sensed that she might be pushing for one. Actually, it was like that with most of the girls I 'date'. A lot of fun teasing, deep conversations, but when it came down to being intimate in body or the heart, I always lose interest. Sigh, I was essentially a playa, but with a social interest in women rather than a physical one. Don't hate the game, the playa's all to blame on this one.

She continues, "A while huh? You must have really been into this girl. Maybe this is a little personal, but why didn't you ever try to date her while she was here?"

"Mostly because she didn't find me attractive, but I don't know. The time just never seemed right. I knew she wasn't interested in me that way, and maybe it's my fault for coming off as an eccentric back then. Then I was struggling to come to terms with it, and when I did ask her if she wanted to go on a date, she got herself a boyfriend. They didn't last long though. Finally, when I wanted to tell her, you know, tell her how I really felt about her, she gets pulled away to another country and I didn't want to make the transition messy for her. So yeah, I guess I blew my chances before I knew what was happening. And I'm talking about this to a complete stranger! No offense. This was not how I expected my day to go."

"Well, if she's not into you, maybe you should just move on? I've liked people before, and when they didn't feel the same way, I stopped losing sleep over them. Yeah, it hurts, but that's life, you know?" What she said made sense, but it wasn't new to me.

"I've thought about it. Actually, when she left, I shaved my head and dove into piles and piles of religious texts, philosophical treatises, anything that might help me deal with the grief of her absence. It made me a lot better at my spiritual studies, so I welcomed the newfound motivation. But over time, I came to accept that this was the way I felt. Then my best friend gets an associate professorship at this university in Tokyo, and now he's there too! It's kinda depressing if you think about it. Japan has a track record of taking away those closest to me."

"Why didn't you just get drunk? Like, a lot! It's a great way to purge. Both your body and your feelings."

"I don't believe in that, it's an abuse of the body. I'm not against others drinking responsibly, but I've downed a bottle of whiskey and would have gagged if not for the coca cola. I don't get drunk in the typical sense anyway, so alcohol really isn't my thing. Drugs either, just in case you get any ideas."

"Okay, but you're missing out on quite the trip. I learn a lot about myself when I have a girls' night out and wake up with a hangover. It's like you said, we need to embrace the chaos that is life."

"Hmmm, maybe you're right… oh damn, it's almost 1 pm! We've been here almost an hour, no wonder the staff keeps giving us dirty looks, we're occupying a four person table and all the business they got from us were two lattes! I have to head back to meet up with a friend for lunch. Um, thanks for listening, Becky, do you need a ride anywhere?"

"No, I'm good, I'm just trying to decide which muffin to get; I swear I'd stuff them all in my mouth but I don't want to overeat. I've got baseball practice in an hour anyway, and the field is quite close, so I'll walk there afterwards."

"Wait, you do baseball? That's very impressive, I didn't think you were the type of person who liked spo – hold up. Do you only like it because the Japanese are into it?"

"At first, yeah. I learned to play a bit while I was in Japan. But I actually like it now. I'd be lying if I said I didn't imagine myself as a less talented Eri Yoshida from time to time."

"…I don't know who she is, sorry."

"She plays for the Toshida Golden Braves. And she was the first girl drafted into a men's baseball team, in 2008, at 16 as well."

"Wow! She. Sounds. Awesome! I'll try to remember her name for Google later. Okay, nice to meet you, *ma ta ne* (see you later)!"

"*Ja ne* (see you), I hope you find what you're missing. Or who!" I smile at her parting shot and make my way back to the counter. I ask them to send her their most tempting platter of dessert muffins, knowing she was likely unable to resist trying a few immediately. She looks surprised as it arrives and glances to me as I make my way out. I send her a look that suggests I am challenging her resolve. She may have thought she was winning our game of social politics, but I wanted to keep things interesting.

Chapter 3

As I drive to meet Oscar at the restaurant, I keep mulling over a new possibility. Becky mentioned she learned more about herself when she tripped out. Maybe I could learn something about myself if I took a trip too, but not with borderline substance abuse. I need to speak with Victor, my best friend, and a man who's known me for the last 12 years. Not on the phone, or via Skype, but in person. And while I'm seeing my best friend, in Japan, I suppose it would be a waste not to see another old friend as well. But first things first, lunch with Oscar.

It is good to see my straightforward and dependable friend after the previous conversation. Lunch is casual, at a fast food place famous for their fried chicken. The setting is almost the complete opposite from what Becky and I shared prior, but I like fast food and its lack of pretentious trappings. Despite franchises like McDonald's trying to gentrify their presentation, the idea of just casually hanging out while enjoying fried goodness is something that strikes a chord in me. Childhood subliminal advertising, perhaps? We'll know in 20 years when my body can no longer process the junk, but my mind is telling me to eat it anyway. I quickly spot him in a booth near the back, and alert him to my presence. He looks up from his game, and away from the endless hordes of undead virtual targets.

"Hey, man, sorry for the delay! I just had coffee with this super intense chick I met at the mindfulness seminar."

"Seriously?"

"Yes." I tell Oscar all about Becky and her mental scanning. He listens with some mild interest, sniggers when

I mention my parting gift, and then I remember why we were here.

"Oh that's right, you've been on weight control for a month! How was the weigh in, good?"

"Good. I made it. And I'm hungrier now that I can finally eat."

"Then let's order a feast and get some meat back on your frame!"

"Okay."

We order a massive bucket with a bunch of sides and do not make conversation until Oscar's has his fill. My poor friend had been on a restrictive diet for the last month, in order to cut weight for his match. Fighters often try to shed as much excess water and fat as possible before a weigh in, thus qualifying them to compete in a lighter (therefore easier?) division. Of course, after checking in their weight, they are free to consume as much as they like. Thus, most fighters are actually heavier than what their bouts would normally permit, but it's something everybody does, so not technically wrong.

Watching him tear through the chicken pieces is disturbingly magnificent, as a pile of bones grows steadily bigger. Halfway through, he slows down the feeding frenzy, allowing his stomach and metabolism to adjust. I pour him a cup of soda, and he nods his thanks as he drains the entire vessel. I refill it. He sips, indicating he has had enough for now.

"So, how's your condition, buddy? Did you see your opponent at the weigh in?"

"Yep, he's shorter, but bulky. Like a walking tree stump. I think I can take him. What about that café girl from earlier? You meeting her again?"

"Hah, I believe you when you say you can take him. Hopefully the match won't go into a decision this time, I know you feel cheated when it does… Nah, I didn't grab her contact details, but I think I have enough to go on if I wanted to find her again. Favourite café, baseball club in the area… I sound like a stalker, don't I?"

"I dunno. She didn't seem to care. But you said she was good at reading you?"

"In my defence, I scanned her pretty good as well. I was more alarmed by the possibility that she was targeting me for being Asian. Though maybe I should give her the benefit of the doubt and not jump to conclusions?"

"Eh, if it attracts girls just use it." Oscar has a point, and to be honest, this wasn't the first girl who expressed an interest in me for my genetics, but she is definitely the most vivacious. Yellow fever runs both ways I suppose.

"There are ethical issues posed with that, my friend. For one, she has a boyfriend. But I also value her opinions more if we weren't involved with each other. You get what I mean?"

"You don't want to bang her?"

"She's cute and sexy in a smart way. But no, I don't want to have a relationship with her."

"You sure you're not gay? You haven't really dated anyone for as far as I can remember. I've dated three people in the time I've known you, not counting casual flings." Oscar and I have known each other for six years, and what he said is true; we met right after Naomi left for Japan. I think back to that night.

We had bonded over a late-night McDonald's brawl, when two guys, drunk and barely out of high school, had gotten into a heated argument with the staff over the ice cream machine being broken. When the staff refused to give them free food, they started knocking over the counter displays and threatening the staff. Maybe it had worked before, somewhere else. The only staff at the counter were two teenage girls and a motherly woman, who I assumed was the manager, and perhaps the boys thought they could get what they wanted with enough intimidation.

Tonight was not their lucky night, as Oscar happened to be on shift, though out of sight. I was about to get up and intervene when, in a flash, Oscar made his way from the drive-through booth and pinned one guy against the wall.

When his friend tried to punch Oscar from behind, I saw a powerfully executed back-kick knock him to the ground. Oscar's attention was divided as the weasel-faced young man he had grabbed was yelling a stream of abuse, a cacophony of whines and squeals. Meanwhile, his friend got up; he was intoxicated, which perhaps lessened the kick's pain, and the leg's power had possibly been diffused due to Oscar grabbing the other guy. I decide to intercept the would-be assailant, before he could charge, spinning him onto his chest and pinning him onto the ground. He was breathing, but did not stir after that. I'm not a fighter, but I know a little kung fu, and was far stronger than most people realised. While I normally resolved issues with words instead of force, this bully gave me the perfect opportunity to vent some of my pent-up feelings. The next part was almost funny, as Oscar's guy repeatedly yet ineffectively tried to head butt his way out of the hold. If only he were sober, he could have seen Oscar's growing annoyance. One real head butt later, followed by a thud, the foolish fellow collapsed. Both of us were reeling from the adrenaline, but things were calmer now. Oscar nodded to me,

"Thanks, but I could have handled it." His voice was deep and steady, but showed appreciation.

"Oh, I believe you. That back kick was superb, considering the position. I was more surprised the other guy didn't stay down." I was exhilarated from the rush, sounding out of breath.

Soon after this, the police arrived and an ambulance had been called too. The paramedics seemed pleased to see that there was no blood, and the boys were taken off somewhere; I didn't pay them further attention. Oscar and the staff were cleaning up and I joined in as much as they allowed me to. We chatted, and I discovered that Oscar was 20, studied politics at the local university, and was heavily involved in mixed martial arts. He learned that I was 23, and a philosopher at heart. Since then we have hung out frequently, becoming fast friends. Maybe it was what we shared on that night, or maybe it was the fact that our different

"Gay? I wish! If I were gay, then all my problems would be solved. But no, I suffer from a romantic abnormality, one so shocking and bizarre that it must be kept hidden from the public at all costs. You see I am attracted to –"

"Stop! I don't want to know." We laugh, as he finishes that Simpsons' quote.

"You know, Oscar, I'm not against giving up meat to join a priesthood. But I have to admit, chicken is one tasty bird."

"I couldn't do it. Meat is life. Literally."

"The spirit is willing, but the flesh is too tempting, huh?"

"Exactly. And I'm not just talking about food either."

We continue with the meal, determined to finish everything on the table. I like chicken, but I love fries. Too much starch for Oscar's taste, but that is perfect as between the both of us we consume the entire table's worth of food.

"Sweet Jesus, I'm stuffed," Oscar tells me as he slouches into his seat.

"Going home soon? The fight's tomorrow morning, right?"

"Yeah, I'm going to take a nap, then do some light training."

"Just watch that knee, you don't want to bust anything right before the match. How are your hands?"

"They're pretty good, actually. The left one is doing a lot better, which makes me more confident." Oscar is a southpaw, despite being right-handed. Apparently, that is pretty common in the world of combat sports.

We make our way out after washing our hands thoroughly to remove the grease of our meal. Sometimes I wonder if we took more care of our hygiene after a meal than before. Hard to think on an empty stomach. Hard to think on a full stomach too, come to think of it. Slowly but surely the food begins to draw blood away from our brains and into our stomachs. Maybe I should take a nap, the caffeine was running out too, but no, the afternoon was young, and I need to make travel plans.

Chapter 4

"Come on you lazy bastard, pick up," I say aloud, as if my best friend could hear me. It's evening, and I have been busy organising flights. I had a reason to wait until this time, as I needed to contact Victor, and he is usually busy until the evenings. Apparently, the Japanese working hours are simply too damn high. It rings a few times, and a woman answers.

"Hey, Thomas! Nice of you to call, what's up?"

"Maggy, my dearest, it's been too long! You look radiant as ever, how's the weather? Cold, right?"

"Oh yeah, we've had a lot of snow lately, it's like a winter wonderland over here. Hang on, let's switch to video call." There's a brief disruption as we both fumble with the touch screen on our respective phones, and then I see her. Margaret, or Maggy as I called her, has porcelain white skin lightly dotted with freckles, and mid-length auburn hair currently tied up in a ponytail. She was classically beautiful, with clean features and a crinkled smile often reserved for the childish antics of her boyfriend and his best friend. Her eyes were amazingly faceted, like sapphires, though depending on the light they also resembled emeralds. I'd compare her to Audrey Hepburn, except she's much more down to earth. The three of us were all the same age, I being slightly older by a month, but she was the de facto matriarchal figure who had to tolerate our nostalgic goofiness.

"So, not that I don't like seeing you, but is Vik around? He normally finishes and comes back around this time, doesn't he?"

"He's just taking a bath right now, but he'll be done soon. Oh, he's coming out. Sigh, with only a towel on…" Maggy's disapproval could not curb the enthusiasm of the new figure who entered the screen. A brilliant toothy smile appeared, enhanced by his richly brown skin, which contrasted with Maggy's. My best friend of 12 years took the phone and lifted it up, forming a downward view, as if to behold my image on his phone.

"Thomas!"

"Vik!"

"Guys! He's going to catch a cold!" Maggy's concern echoes through the speakers, though it does little to curb our elation. All the same I know that she's right, my friend is prone to chills and I'm not sure how heated their apartment is.

"Yes, Miss Fitzwilliams!" She is right, I think, as I playfully act like a sheepish schoolboy caught passing notes in class. I respect her position as a teacher, but that does not mean I was above teasing her about it. Vik can be heard frantically drying himself off properly, the noise of blow-drying adds a rushed ambience as we continue speaking.

"So, Thomas, what have you been up to?"

"Oh, you know, just critiquing the human condition. I gave a small talk to a mindfulness seminar earlier today actually, so that was cool."

"Wow, nice! How's that girl you were seeing, uh, Ashley? The one who did classical Chinese dancing."

"Oh, Hailey? No, I haven't spoken to her in months. She wanted to focus on her dancing, so I figured she wasn't that into me. Her loss. But fear not, I am still sampling the delights of bachelordom! Plus there's always Internet porn, can't go wrong there, can I?"

"Hmmm," Maggy smiles, because despite becoming stricter as a teacher these days, she's still someone I consider one of the guys. "Yes, I'm sure that you don't spend too much time on that part of the web, do you?"

"Uhhh… No? But when I do, please know that I am properly ashamed of myself!" We have a good laugh at the implications of my tone. Vik returns, now fully dressed, and rugged up in a green and blue sweater.

"Are we talking about porn? Come on guys, you could have waited for me! So what, is Thomas into some really kinky stuff now?!" Spontaneously, I decide to simulate oral sex with the camera, my mouth a chasm that grows larger and smaller and I rock my head backwards and forwards. Vik sees this and copies me, which we all have a good time giggling about it as the video shakes. Maggy regains her composure first, unsurprisingly.

"Are you two done?!"

"Thanks, Maggy, you are a saint to put up with us. Actually, now that you're both here, I can tell you some good news: I'll be visiting real soon!" Vik and Maggy gasp, as I tell them I will be visiting in a few days.

"No way, that's amazing! Well, you can stay with us, we have a spare futon you can sleep on. Although, before committing anymore, how long are you staying?"

"Actually, that's the thing, I'm training and bussing my way from Tokyo all the way to Osaka. A few major stops in-between. I'd hate to make you feel unspecial, but there's plenty of other people I'm seeing too, lots of important meetings, etcetera, etcetera. But don't feel bad, you guys are the first on my list! As I'm only there for a week, we could spend a whole Sunday together, before I leave on Monday morning."

"What!? A week only, and you're only seeing me for a day? Come on man, doesn't our friendship deserve more!?" Vik is pleading with me to stay longer.

"A week is all I can spare, I have to get back in time for my birthday. There's something heavy going on."

Sensing that the mood is changing to a more serious one, Maggy tactfully excuses herself so that Vik and I can have our privacy. While we do enjoy juvenile fun and heaps of nostalgia, Vik and I have stayed friends for over a decade. The only way that would be possible is if we actually grew as individuals too, accepting the other. As we matured into adulthood, he has been my most trusted confidante; our platonic love would put most married couples to shame, though Maggy has never seemed threatened by it. If getting his PhD didn't destroy them, I doubt anything short of cheating could.

"So, bro, what's up? Even for you, coming to Japan on a moment's notice isn't normal." He is calmly attentive now, matching my expression. I tell him about the conversation with my parents, all about my fears and indecision concerning life, and I even mention what Becky said to me earlier. He then addresses something which I have told few people about: my unresolved feelings.

"You're finally going to see Naomi."

"Yes. I want to see her again. I still have to let her know I'm coming, but I'll do it after this." I laugh nervously, trying to cover my insecurities. Vik had met her, of course, and had been a willing source of support through the roughest parts of my loneliness and dejection.

"How do you know she's still even in Osaka?"

"We talk online, every now and then. I think I may be the only one of her old group who still does."

"Obviously you haven't forgotten her, but, I mean, what do you hope to accomplish? She didn't like you then, what's changed now?"

"I just want to know how I feel about her now. I need to know, and soon. Maybe things have changed, and when I see her, talk to her again after all this time, maybe it will make it easier to let go. Or who knows, maybe deep down I'm hoping she'll feel differently about me, but honestly, that scares me more! I don't know what kind of relationship we could have, and I may even be a priest in another month! It's fine, it's fine, and a part of me wants to do it, finally, but it just feels like everything is moving so fast and I can't tap into my centre of balance… it's like being a teen again!"

"Woah, it's kinda weird hearing you be so vulnerable… I mean, look, you're clearly still head over heels for Naomi. Yet you don't know why – hang on, yes baby?!" Maggy had said something indiscernible in the background, and Vik was asking her to repeat herself. *She doesn't like that*, I smirk inwardly. I'm not sure if it's appropriate, but I do like it when they bicker at times, almost like an old married couple. I find it cute, heart-warming even. Will I find that for myself one day?

"Okay, sorry, Thomas, I gotta cut this short. Maggy's prepared a late dinner, was waiting for me to get home, and you know what she's like when she's hungry." I nod knowingly.

"Godspeed. Put her on and I'll say bye together!" Another moment of scuffling as he makes his way to their dining room. The sound of sliding doors can be heard, which I figure is to save on heating. I put on a cheery disposition.

"Sorry for holding you up, Maggy! Enjoy dinner, I'll see you both by the end of the week!"

"Thanks for calling, Thomas, can't wait to see you!"

"Bye bye, love you, Vik!" I admit, I like to think Maggy gets jealous when we openly display our affection, but realistically a part of her probably enjoys it.

"*Oyasumi* (goodnight), love you, Thomas!"

The screen goes dark, I am disconnected by phone as well as from my emotions. Taking a deep breath, I open Facebook Messenger, and scroll through my contacts until I find her. The last message we exchanged was a few months ago, when she told me about her trek up Mt Fuji. She had gone with a special group in the middle of the night, so that they would arrive in time to see the sunrise. It sounded majestic, and the photos proved so.

Thomas: Hey Naomi, I hope you are doing well and looking after yourself. I'm going to Japan to see my best friend soon. I fly out in a few days, arriving on Sunday in Tokyo. I'll be travelling through several cities and I'm in Osaka on Friday/Saturday. If you have time, wanna meet up?

Although our conversations usually consisted of delays between responses, I must have gotten lucky this time: I saw her typing a message a few seconds after I sent mine.

Naomi: Are you really comingggg?

            I'm free, I think, lol.

            Let's meet up??

Thomas: Awesome let's have lunch together! You
            can show me your favourite place hahah.

Naomi: hahaha, too many. But we'll figure it out
            closer to then, okay??

Thomas: Sure, no problem lol. Goodnight Naomi!

Naomi: Can't wait, byeee!

The relief I feel is indescribable. She seemed pleased that I was coming to see her too. It is as if no time has passed whatsoever since I saw her in person. Feeling my head clear a little, I drop into bed and try to settle into oblivion.

Chapter 5

A few days later, I am out of the country, waiting inside Singapore's Changi Airport. It is a place I have been to a handful of times before, when travelling internationally, but it seems bigger since the last time I passed through. I've read that it is an ideal location for international stopovers, and that the country runs like clockwork. My friends who lived there, enlightened me to the other aspects of this city-sized country: fines and queues. Chewing gum is illegal too, though it was a soft contraband which I had occasionally picked out from the crowds whilst visiting said friends a few years ago. This time I am just on a stopover and flying out to Narita Airport in three hours. My luggage is surprisingly light, for all I have is my cabin bag, a small suitcase filled with creature comforts Vik and Maggy have requested, and a gift for Naomi. I daresay I am travelling light because the true bulk of my cargo is carried in my heart.

The whole planning process was a surprisingly smooth one. Explaining my intentions to the flight agent, Jerry, I discovered that Japan didn't require tourist visas for the length of my stay, and while I travelled across Honshu, the main island, I could get a JR (Japan Rail) pass. The JR pass was something visitors to the country could apply for, a one-week permit to ride almost any of the trains. It cost several hundred dollars, but considering the amount of travelling in store, it would probably save me around the same amount. I have to admit, I was looking forward to the winter season once I arrive there. My fashion sense is geared towards colder climates, and I have a good deal of natural resistance to such weather too. Of course, right now, in Singapore, I was lucky to be indoors with air conditioning, something anyone who has visited the area will agree with. Not that the country gets particularly hot, compared to home, but the humidity results in a dense air that takes some getting used to, and I like breathing air that doesn't make me feel fat.

"Thomas!" I am alerted to a young man with prominent features, and as he approaches, I recognise who had called out to me.

"Jake, is that really you? You cut your hair, it looks good!" It is an old friend of mine. He is much younger than me, about seven years if I recall correctly.

"Yes, your number 1 disciple is here, it must be fate!" I laugh at our inside joke.

"It's a wonder to see you here, of all places! And I told you already, I'm not good enough to be anyone's master, least of all a talented young man such as yourself."

I smile fondly, recalling when this energetic young man and I first became acquainted. A few years ago, I had given a speech at a university about the nature of oneness in Tao, relating it to the monad or henosis of Western philosophy. I addressed my own views on the topic, about the nature of Mind, Body and Spirit, and how it was essential to work towards bridging the gap between these three. The idea was that, in time, Thought, Action and Feelings would occur as a single true expression of Self, rather than independent collaborative actions.

Afterwards I spoke to Jake, then a long-haired teenager who practised aikido, one of Japan's joint manipulation styles. His pursuit of lore relevant to Ai Ki, the principle of universal love overcoming resistance, was impressive, and had led him to my little talk in the first place. Not just interested in theory, he took his training seriously, and augmented it with detailed historical research about anything related to Japanese martial arts. My lecture, though unintentional, pointed him to some new directions to explore. Over time, and many discussions, he had come to gain some perspective and insight based on my philosophical views. Calling me 'Master' was a sign of his appreciation. I have always been touched, though I also always remind him that he was too good to be my disciple.

"It's good to see you again, Thomas! Are you heading to Japan too?" Taking a closer look at him, I notice that he is wearing thick clothing, a sturdy-looking parka on top of the trousers and sweater. I look at myself in comparison. I decided to wear my classic look, which is not a business suit, but black trousers, top, and my iconic black long coat. Along with a scarf, and my glasses, I didn't seem out of place for Japan either.

"Yes, good guess! Tokyo?" He nods and explains that he had trained diligently in aikido for the past few years. Now he would be travelling to stay with Yoseikan Dojo in Shizuoka province. This practice was common enough with old-school styles too, and as a live-in student, he would be expected to help the instructors with administration, maintenance and basically anything requested of him, in addition to frequent training. Such students would normally have to find work to support themselves, but Jake explains that he is only there for an intensive month, and his family has funded him as a gift. He then asks me what I'm doing in Japan.

"Oh, I'm seeing friends. It's my birthday soon, and I figured that I may as well usher the final year of my 20s in style and a change of scenery!"

"Hah, that's awesome! You should come visit me in Shizuoka if you get the chance, I think the instructors there will be happy to see you in action!"

"You must be joking, I don't even do aikido! They'll think I'm deliberately insulting the school! Hahah, come on, we've got time before the flight, let's grab a snack somewhere."

We wander through the airport, which is essentially a small city's smaller city. There are plenty of duty-free items for sale, and the entire place has been upgraded since I last visited, with a new food court as well as a butterfly exhibit. Walking into the latter reminds us of Singapore's climate, and we quickly exit on account of being too over-dressed.

Eventually it is time to board, and by good fortune, we are able to swap our original seats and stay together for our seven-hour long flight, which does not seem as long now. Good company truly does make all the difference.

Chapter 6

We make it to Narita Airport, safe and sound. The arrivals sector is very futuristic (from my humble perspective), with the most efficient check out system I've ever been processed by. There is even an infections gate that scans body temperature, to weed out any viral threats coming into Japan. I head out, cleared by each stop point, though at the declarations gate, the officer is particularly interested in why I have so many kinds of chocolate. A gift, I explain, and he smiles knowingly. Surprisingly good grasp of English by the airport staff, though I guess it's to be expected.

Jake, being a tall and sinewy young man, didn't come off the airplane as fresh as I did (my body being shorter and having more biological padding). I see Vik and Maggy waiting for me, dressed very snugly, and our reunion creates warmth that contrasts with the weather.

"Thomas! Thomas, Thomas, Thomas! I can't believe it, you're finally here!" My best friend and I embrace with emotional depth that as only two straight men can achieve. Maggy watches on, clearly amused at our display. Vik continues, "Well, it took us more than 10 years, but we can finally say we've met up in another country!"

"Yes, though the wait was long, surely I was worth it? Team Panda is back! Hahahah!" Team Panda was our trio's nickname, coined by the literary pundit yours truly. To think that an animal could exist as simultaneously Black, White and Asian, remarkable!

"Awww, even your laugh is the same! No one laughs like that here! Hey, who's your friend?"

I quickly introduce Jake to the group, and he is welcomed warmly. Maybe Maggy feels a kindred spirit in another Caucasian, especially as her time is now predominantly spent with people who aren't. It is less a matter of race and more about sociological identity. I, who grew up as an Asian in a Caucasian environment, could understand the difficulties of belonging in such circumstances. Although, come to think of it, back home Maggy's circle of friends was actually quite diverse, so I might just be over thinking it.

Jake is scheduled to rendezvous with a group of aikido practitioners later. But until then, he is welcome to join us, and seems ecstatic when Maggy informs him we are visiting a local Samurai Museum. My tour guides think I will enjoy it, and they are right, but my enthusiasm is nothing compared to Jake's. We make our way to the airport train station, where Jake and I spend a few minutes collecting our JR passes from a small office. Then we follow our informal guides to the correct tracks; I openly admit that I would have gotten lost if left alone, as I have little by way of a sense of direction. Yet I'll never forget my first impression of Tokyo City.

It is magical to walk out and see the pure white snow covering the landscape, though the streets and footpaths are mostly clear. I don't know if it is the accumulated fatigue, or just the Tokyo rhythm, but Victor and Margaret are walking at double the pace Jake and I am. I need to actively speed up, otherwise my body would slow down considerably. I'm not really tired though, that much I'm certain of, as the power naps on the flights over have helped. Even without the benefit of light sleep, it doesn't matter: I am now in Tokyo! The crisp cold air clears my head, and I relish the thought of heading out with old friends to an actual samurai museum. I feel like I'm on a movie set too, with all the different sights, and smells and sounds, all around, surrounding me as I breathe in the city air. Even traffic lights played a beat to usher people across the streets! I'm in Japan, and I'm loving every second of the experience.

It became clear to us soon that the JR pass was not an all-access pass. On the subway, an officer on duty kindly points out that subways are not trains… so we proceed to fiddle with the ticket machines before seeing a button that reads 'English Menu'. That made things easier, but we still took a moment to work out how our fares were paid. Yen is not a bad currency, but I have to point out that its fondness for coinage made for a very jingle-jangle transition (there were 3 or 4 types of notes, and double the variety of coins).

Other things that become apparent, as I drink in the sights, are a seemingly endless amount of convenience stores ('Konbinni' as they are known), and vending machines in abundance. These commonplace features permeate the landscape, but grow endearing over time. It could have been the novelty of seeing them as part of my first impression, or maybe I simply biased from the neural cocktail my brain was swimming in; I feel as if I'm a kid again, with unchecked wonder and unashamed joy. I smile at everything and everyone. Many folks are wearing white face masks, yet more often than not I see my smile being returned, albeit more conservatively. The masks are commonplace in Japan, as Vik and Maggy explain. In addition to filtering the air, they serve to act as protection from the elements in winter, something that didn't occur to me due to my cold weather resistance. I wonder, how could anyone want to dilute these refreshing blasts entering their lungs?

For this reason, I'm mildly disappointed when we traverse the labyrinth that is public transportation lines, as another amenity is discovered; the seats are heated here! Even I, who preferred cool temperatures, can appreciate the thoughtfulness and comforting nature of this innovation. Everywhere I look around, the people are composed and orderly, the streets are all clean and I sense that everyone understands the value of individual contribution towards a better society… Okay, I'm done giving oral to Japan. I have to use a bathroom, so I excuse myself once we arrive in Shinjuku.

I have to take back what I said, about curbing my praise for the Japanese, because even the toilets here are a masterpiece! Clean and definitely did not feel as if it were used by many people prior, kind of like a high-class hooker. Forgive me, that was uncalled for. How dare I compare this marvel to a prostitute?! I would pay to use a toilet like this, and even though I am a little intimidated by the extra functions, a helpful sign was able to show me the basics. This reminds me of a few years ago, when I became a casual foodie. Rather than post on Instagram (which I only did a handful of times), I decided to review restaurants, and added my own unique twist: the score I gave included a bathroom review section. Nothing tasteless, just a general score given to cleanliness, décor and overall impression. There were many soul-crushing disappointments, and I feel as if many did not do their restaurant justice. However, there were some fabulous bathroom concepts as well; one seafood restaurant had an aquarium in theirs! So I suppose my opinions on these Japanese bathrooms carried slightly more weight, but it's hard to feel superior when I think about how hardworking these toilets are. Seats are automatically warmed, and the walls show not a trace of dilapidation, something unfathomable at a typical Western train station bathroom. I wonder, how much it would cost to buy one? I make a mental note to ask Vik and Maggy later.

It is only a short walk to the Samurai Museum from the station. I pick up very quickly that walking must be an integral part of the daily commute, and maybe this was how my friends had gotten so proficient. Maggy was definitely no slouch, but when we hung out back home, she and Vik took a more casual stroll. Here, without even trying, their slowest setting seems brisk by comparison! I want to enjoy my sightseeing, as the architecture of Japan has more personality that I'm used to. Small shops with a classic look somehow manage to complement the skyscrapers and multi-platform shopping areas, and there is no lack of eateries. It's still relatively early, about 11 am, but my friends ask us if we are hungry.

"I'm not, how about you, Jake?" He shakes his head before responding.

"Nah, I'm still a little full from the airline food." Maggy then looks at her phone, checking the website for information regarding tour times.

"It says here that the next tour group is at 11:30 am, lasts until around 1 pm. Are you sure you're okay waiting?" Jake and I both nod, being more interested in the building before us than food.

The Samurai Museum is two storeys high, in a more traditional architectural style, featuring sliding wood-framed doors. There is even a full set of crimson red samurai armour located at the front door! I marvel at how small the ancient Japanese had to be, until I realise that the armour only went down to one's knees, and once you account for the rest of the legs, their height would have been more or less normal We walk in, and see a small crowd gathered near reception. Maggy, always practical, goes to buy our tickets instead of gawking at the displays. In our defence, there's a certain psychology involved with boys and swords, so we can't be blamed for our distraction. Plus, as Jake points out, many of the displays are actual sets and not replicas. Amazing, I'm standing right next to something that many had probably fought and died in, and is now being exhibited for tourists hundreds of years later. A young lady with red highlights in her hair motions for the group to gather. She is our tour guide, very brightly presented, and speaks good English despite an accent; we are composed of westerners as well as non-local Asians (likely not Japanese), with Vik being the only black guy in the crowd.

"Hello everybody! Welcome to the Tokyo Samurai Museum. My name is (she gives it to us, though I can't recall it), but you can just call me Mio!" Her bright and cute demeanour brings smiles to all our faces, and we soon discover that she is good at her job. As we explore the ground level, we become conscious of space, as the exhibits here are located on either side of a pebbled pathway. Many of us did not know if it is appropriate to step onto to the gravelly floor off the path, but everyone manages to settle into a good spot as we listen to her speak. Mio explains that samurai were the nobility class of warriors, and reveals that the armour we see being exhibited belonged to the richest and most powerful of their time. I am familiar with Japanese history (having studied the Sengoku era until the Meiji era) but it is wonderful to be reminded of names I had not needed to remember after passing their subject exams. A brochure allows even those unfamiliar with Japanese history to keep up as she mentions dates and historical figures, namely Nobunaga, Tokugawa, and Hideoyoshi.

Mio is funny without trying to be overtly so. For instance, she explains how Nobunaga was a great warlord who almost succeeded in unifying Japan, but he was a 'mean boss', so his subordinates killed him before he could accomplish that feat. We learn that armours were meant as political statements as well as military protection. One of the sets displayed here used bearskin from China, merely to demonstrate the fact that his family could afford bearskin from China. I was curious about the ornate, almost peacocking features on the helmets. Mio explains that the ancient Japanese were shorter, probably owing to less meat in their diet, so many leaders aimed to make themselves more intimidating with large helmet displays. Their partially shaven heads were to account for how hot the splendid armours became, and it goes without saying that the attire got heavy too, after a day on the battlefield. Our attention is then directed to a large mural painting, depicting a very famous scene: the battle of Sekigahara in the 16th century. Our guide once again charms us with her funny trivia of the scene.

"As you are seeing, this is the battle of Sekigahara, which took place in Osaka. Just a replica though, the real one is in Osaka Castle. Osaka used to be the old capital of Japan, until the Tokugawa Shogunate established itself in Edo, in 1603. In this corner, you can see the men fleeing from the battle, having lost. In the corner, there are several men in various stages of seppuku, ritual suicide. Death by disembowelment was actually slow and painful, so that's why you also see men with swords ready to decapitate those who commit seppuku. Now, why are there so many clouds in the picture, you may ask? Simple, the artist who drew it became lazy and didn't care anymore." We all have a good laugh at that. An American man proceeds to ask if this was the same battle in the opening of the movie 'Musashi'. Any fan of Japanese swordsmanship would immediately recognise that name: Minamoto Mushashi was a legendary swordsman, though Jake had explained a curious backstory to me about a soldier who wanted to be a general, not a duellist, yet ended up with such a legacy. True to form, my knowledgeable friend interjects,

"Actually, this may not have been where Musashi was during Sekigahara. There was another battle being fought at the same time, in that area, so sources can't really say one way or another."

The crowd, and guide, in particular, are taken by his contribution. Taking advantage of the discussion topic, Mio explains that to us that Musashi was regarded as a great fighter, but distinctly not a samurai, who were of established lineage. We then head to the second floor and are asked to remove our shoes before entering (not surprising to me, as I am Asian too). There are pigeonholes to store our foot ware, along a wall. Of course, there is also more armour displayed here. Mio continues her tour: we see a collection of different weaponry, such as swords, a bow that is bigger than she, and even old guns. She explains that Japan has two distinct swords, the tachi and the katana. To reiterate the point she made earlier about Musashi's prowess, she also mentions that it took decent strength to wield one effectively, yet the legendary swordsman used two in combat, forming the prototype of dual wielding. Thus, it could be concluded that the man was very strong as well as skilled, all the more inflating his status in popular culture.

"You see that the armour here is a little different. Why? The answer is behind us: guns. Old armours downstairs were designed for arrows and blades. But trading with the Portuguese introduced firearms to Japan, and once guns became common in battle, the armour was changed to reflect this."

We move to a different section now, and it becomes clear that time is moving forwards a few hundred years. We see that the Tokugawa administration sealed off Japan until the 1850s, when the arrival of U.S. Commodore Perry forced Japan to reconsider its closed-door policy. Then the civil war erupted between the Imperialists, who wanted to open Japan to the world, and the Shogunate, which aimed to keep things as they were, resulting in the end of the Edo Period and the start of the Meiji era in 1868. We see the impact of Western civilisation, but I also see uniforms of the Shinsengumi, special police force of the Tokugawa Shogunate, and am more drawn to those. I do not practice Japanese martial arts, much less their swordsmanship, but I was fascinated by the idea of the Shinsengumi, particularly Captain Hajime Saito. I'm glad that most modern depictions show him as a decently handsome man; historical sources indicate otherwise. I feel that if someone couldn't be attractive in life, then at least there's some comfort in being posthumously remembered as such.

The tour is coming to an end soon, but we are all offered a chance to wear different outfits, for photo opportunities. I jump at the chance to put on the outer robes of a Shinsengumi uniform, complete with headband too. Ah, I suppose wish fulfilment is not so bad, if any police force still employed such uniforms, I would have signed up years ago. Vik and Maggy put on a beautiful set of brocade robes, brilliantly flowing vermillion for Maggy, and a handsome dark blue set for Vik. The attire matched them, I swear they seemed to generate their own little bubble as I took the picture. Truly a picture-perfect moment.

My own photos are nothing impressive, as usual, but I also try on a samurai helmet and face mask. To our surprise and amusement, they fit me perfectly, facial structure and all, so I didn't even need to tie it on. Poor Jake though, the helmet kept slipping over his eyes when he tried it on. It was mentioned earlier that Darth Vader's appearance was based on samurai armour, and I was able to envision how intimidating we would look to those who did not know us. Precisely the look George Lucas was going for when designing the character? Jake and Mio had struck up a conversation, mostly about his own knowledge of Japanese history. I smile inwardly – like most straight guys, Jake has a fondness for pretty women. Mio may be a little older than him, but that could be a good thing; dating an older woman was very educational, or so I've heard. Suddenly, Jake is excited by something she said, and Mio repeats it for the four of us.

"In about 20 minutes, we have a live samurai demonstration in the room next door. It is open to the public, would you like to come along and see?" Naturally we are all very eager and wait around downstairs for the event to start. To pass the time, we browse through the gift shop and explore the various wares. It is really more of a gift room, as there are no doors: it is essentially a box with one open side acting as the entrance/exit. Swords and other samurai memorabilia are lined against the wall, all for sale, along with keychains and various novelties. I notice a selection of coin purses, which remind me of the handful I have been storing in my pockets. Jake is immersed in the small book collection in the corner, while I consider buying myself a replica men-gu (the facemask I had tried on earlier). It was a good replica, as in 30,000 Yen good. Too good for me, unfortunately. I wander back to Vik and Maggy, just outside of the shop entrance.

"Are you doing okay, Thomas? You must be feeling hungry by now?" Maggy expresses concern at how thin my face seems, but I assure her that it was no big deal to wait until we are done here.

"Well, the entire demo only takes half an hour apparently, and there're lots of really nice places all around here."

"Thanks, Maggy, what would we do without you?" My playful tones convince her that I am doing alright, and we all chat about everything we've seen so far, until it is time to head back upstairs for the exhibit. It is cramped, but there are floor cushions which take up about half the room. We take a seat in the back corner. Unlike most of the audience, Jake and I are kneeling instead of sitting cross-legged; he does so because he knows it is the Japanese way, and I do it because my legs go numb otherwise. The room thickens as more people arrive, and we begin to squish closer, maximising every inch of space. A small group of elderly Japanese men gather at the back, next to me. Typically polite, they excuse themselves, as if they were intruding upon my space.

"Ah, *sumemasen* (pardon me)!" an older man with full head of hair flecked with grey sits down next to me.

"*Mo, daijoubu* (it's fine)," I smile in reply. He then mentions something to me, but as I did not speak Japanese I could only apologise with the few broken phrases I knew.

He looks mildly surprised, but considering how I was dressed and sitting, as well as initially using my limited Japanese, it might have been my fault. Then he laughs, and replies in clear English,

"No problem." I laugh as well, the awkwardness dissipating as acceptance bridges the language gap. A side door opens, and the crowd hushes expectantly. To everyone's surprise, two toddlers wander through, followed by their parents. The older gentlemen next to me exclaims,

"Ah, samurai!" Everyone bursts into laughter, and the presenter plays along. He is a round but sturdy looking, about my age, and presents in English for the benefit of the crowd.

"Ladies and gentlemen, just to be clear, these toddlers will not be fighting for us today!" Another chorus of laughter runs through the crowd. The door opens again, and this time it is obviously the samurai. We clap, and the man looks on solemnly for a moment, before turning and heading back out. We are stunned, until the presenter tells us that maybe he will come back if we cheered louder, which we do. The samurai pops his head back in and smiles, clearly having used this gimmick many times in his career. I recall that this type of slapstick was very popular during the mid-1900s in South East Asia, but I am partial to the occasional slapstick so am enjoying his entrance.

However, it is soon obvious that this man is not just an actor: I could see how fluid and practical his transitions are, as he begins to take several poses with his katana. We watch in awe as he draws, slashes and almost parries the very air we breathe, demonstrating his skill. Then, a golden opportunity arrives. The presenter asks for two volunteers to come forward, and Jake immediately places his hand up. I also motion for him to be chosen, hoping to increase his chances. I think it helped, because Jake *is* picked, along with a lightly cocoa-skinned girl (maybe Indian?) They are introduced to the basic method of drawing a sword from the scabbard, and the difference in skill became immediately apparent to all of us watching, especially the samurai; Jake had never been known for slacking off in his training. In one instance of a downward slash, I see the blade warp (slightly) under the force! Jake gets a little carried away when the two volunteers are asked to Ki-ai (shout while exhaling). It is powerful, and even causes one of the small boys from earlier to start crying! But everyone has a good laugh, clapping enthusiastically.

When it is all over, Jake asks for a photo while striking a pose with the man. The presenter translates questions from the audience, explaining that this man came from a school which was famous for their moves being incorporated in movie choreography. No wonder, those moves were very authentic looking, and you couldn't just stage that genuine factor.

We leave the museum in good spirits and with a good appetite. The question now is, where to eat? Every street we see is paved with different restaurants that offer formal and casual options. At last we decide on ramen noodles and enter a place Vik has tried before. Some doors in Japan are semi-automatic – you press a button to trigger them, rather than rely on a sensor. This feature has resulted in me almost stepping into the door, and subsequently ripping them off the hinges. Thankfully, despite some fatigue, I still have enough wits about me to realise how it works, before looking too much like a lost foreigner.

A delicious hearty aroma of broth and other dishes washes over us the moment we step inside, and fortunately we locate a booth big enough for four people after placing our order. There is a system in place that is essentially a touch-screen menu and also allows you to pay. Not by card though, it is strictly cash only. Something one has to get used to Japan is that a lot of transactions are cash based. This particular establishment doesn't take notes greater than 5,000 yen, but our total meal of four ramen bowls, two plates of karaage (fried chicken) and a side of gyoza (fried dumplings) barely amounts to 4,000 yen. I flip open my wallet in a flash and pull out a 5,000 note, despite the protests of my guides. I may be a guest in their country, but I know how to show gratitude. Maggy and Vik had insisted on covering the museum, so it was only fair, and Jake was essentially my disciple so it wasn't out of the ordinary for me to treat him to a meal.

After taking a seat, I am delighted to see iced water for our consumption. Even though it is chilly outside, it appears as if the Japanese agree with my taste for cold water, no matter the season, and especially when enjoying hot meals. I sip gratefully, for I had not realised how dehydrated I had become. The dishes arrive soon after we sit down, and I am once again impressed with the efficiency. I remove the pork rasher from my bowl, giving it to Vik, who is an avid lover of meat. Sifting through the broth, the steam coyly makes my mouth water. With a curved spoon I sample the soup, a rich and subtle blend of stocks and seasonings. Slightly salty, slightly sweet, entirely appealing and welcome in my stomach. The noodles are cooked well, not too soft but with just the right amount of chewiness that makes for a satisfying ramen experience. Along with gentle bursts of flavour from the mushrooms and bamboo shoots, my first ramen in Japan lives up to the hype.

The fried chicken is different to what I expected. Karaage I've tried were typically small pieces of crunchy goodness, but these are the size of fillets. Vik explains to me that this place was atypical, as virtually every other restaurant he tried had served what I typically consider karaage. Flavour-wise it is still succulent and as tasty as any I've had, with a rounded dose of seasoning used in the crumb coating. I do not try the gyoza dumplings, but they look fresh, and I can imagine that the stuffed fillings would have been a treat, if I had more of an appetite. Vik asks me,

"So, Thomas, how is it? Good?" I'm chewing, my mouth is full of noodles, so I cannot respond except by nodding vigorously. After swallowing, I do reply properly.

"Yeah, it's great, thanks for taking me here. Is this place a franchise or just a stand-alone shop?"

"Er, I think it's a franchise, there's quite a few of them here. But there are also plenty of family restaurants here, and they aren't in a rush to faze them out. Maybe the business is good, from tourists as well as locals. The work hours are pretty full on, so most single people aren't up to cooking, especially if they work a corporate job."

That remark makes me think of Naomi. Is she overworked? Does she look after herself? I know she is capable but still I wonder! Is she eating and sleeping properly? Does she have anyone to look after her if she falls ill? Oh no, am I a bad friend for not knowing??? I regain my composure before continuing to chat with Vik,

"Oh yeah. That's convenient I suppose. Oh, I recall that medication is really controlled here. As requested, I have played your drug mule and gotten a few things past customs."

"Thanks, Thomas, it was sure nice of you to risk Japanese prison for me. You definitely dodged being someone's bitch, for sure!"

"Hah, I see you clearly need these meds, for in prison I am no one's bitch!" We joke around, knowing full well that I did nothing illegal. I had brought over a small amount of anti-histamines and a box of over the counter analgesics. All declared at the airport, so there definitely wasn't anything shady about what I had done. I try to tease him, switching to a more playful demeanour.

"It is a shame that you are so weak as to need them. I came to Japan with the clothes on my back, and my everyday carry bag. All the suitcase stuff? It's yours." Vik plays along.

"Yes, but unfortunately I don't quite have your 'insulation'. I'm sure that if I had such 'ample reserves' I would not need extra clothing either!"

"Hey! I'll have you know I went to the gym every day in the week before coming here! I even got my six-pack back: wanted to look good for my xiong di!"

"I bet you wanted to look good for someone!"

We laugh again, though mine is partially out of embarrassment. Vik and I had no secrets, for the most part. He knows how important Naomi is to me, and thankfully does not continue that line of conversation as we are in public. One by one, we finish eating and make our way out. An American tourist asks us for change; he only has a 10,000 yen note and couldn't buy ramen due to the currency cap on those machines. Vik deftly swaps him two 5,000-yen notes, and the guy is now able to purchase a good meal. Instead, he goes outside to buy cigarettes from a vending machine. I suppose he is going to eat after a smoke. I also consider buying some cigarettes, but Vik tells me that it is probably cheaper, and better quality, to buy at any shop, so we continue along our journey. For the record, I don't smoke, but for personal reasons I do like the idea of carrying a pack with me.

Our next stop: Edo Castle! It is quite majestic even from a distance, but unfortunately we do not go inside, as Edo Castle is closed today. Funnily enough, it was open every other day except today. That's ironic timing for you. But we make the most of a good situation, taking in the scenery as we walk around the moat for a while. Even in this season, there are plenty of joggers, including a whole team of runners dressed in blue tracksuits. Instead of expressing how disappointed we are, we are grateful to be in the vicinity, and make our way on foot towards Akihabara, a district famous for anime as well as general pop-culture. The streets are flooded with everything an enthusiast could want! There are robot maid cafés, schoolgirls handing out flyers (well, ages aside, they were dressed as schoolgirls), plenty of shopping opportunities, and lots of anime-based advertising, even on the buildings! Jake had to leave us soon, he was meeting up with another group bound for Shizuoka, Kanagawa. They were taking a bus in about an hour, which I noted were a longer but cheaper alternative to the bullet trains. I tease him about getting a massage from one of the many parlours we pass by. He says that he doesn't want to be seedy on the first day he arrives, but I also point out that over here the massage parlours are likely to be just massage parlours; there was even a sign with an express disclaimer, **"Our clothes stay on!"**

I find it funny but then look around more carefully to see whether or not I can detect any forms of exploitation. Maggy had explained to me that at certain times during the night, there were female exclusive trains, to prevent unsolicited groping from perverts (the male ones anyway), which I found mildly shocking as it reminded me of the darker underbelly present within each society. Still, as I can't immediately detect anything shady going on, I decide to just enjoy these sights at face value.

We enter a store that catches our eye, and I find myself looking at a simple dark-blue and white yukata. I used to think that kimonos were for girls while yukatas were for guys, but I now know that they are general styles of clothes which cater for both men and women. Jake finds himself a pair of geta, Japanese wooden shoes, that he falls in love with, though they cost about 5,000 yen. My yukata is about 4,000, once tax is factored in. With my limited grasp on the local language, I'm able to interact with the elderly service lady, who explains which sizes I would probably need, considering my build.

In this country, prices do not automatically include tax, so I'm glad to be proficient at mental math, which allowed me to calculate costs more precisely. Maggy finds herself a beautifully crafted wooden jewellery box, which she allows me to pay for, as foreigners visiting Japan are granted tax-exempt status for purchases over 5,000 yen. I'm pleased, glad to do something for a friend, and this only sweetens the deal for us. The shop staff knows a little English, though at this place they also speak Mandarin. I find it comforting, as despite being woefully bad at it, I understand more of that than Japanese. However, transactions only occur in English. It's an unwritten rule in retail that the customer and the staff would only be understood when they are addressed, allowing the illusion of privacy, especially when multilingualism is a factor. At least, when I worked in retail that was what I learned, and the same principles should still apply even though that was over 10 years ago. As we leave, I hand Maggy her gift item.

"Thanks, Thomas, let me pay you back?"

"No no, I insist, you've been a wonderful tour guide! It's the least I can do." She smiles and accepts my gift, knowing me too well to bother arguing.

Jake takes his leave from our group and separates from us at the station as we head to different platforms. He was going to meet his team at the bus port. I wish him well.

"Good luck over there! I'll come visit on Wednesday to see how you do! Send me the address and everything later! Stay warm, don't catch a chill!"

"Yes, master!" Jake leaves us and I watch him disappear around the corner. Vik and Maggy lead me to the platform that heads to Zushi. It isn't a long ride, and we are silent on the way back, letting the events of the day wash over us as I process my debut in Japan.

Chapter 7

We make it to Zushi Station and proceeded to walk to a place Vik highly recommended; I'm going to try my first okonomiyaki in Japan. We make our way to a family-owned business about three floors high, not that far from Zushi Station. Owing to the time, dinner rush hour is over and we easily find a table. Okonokiyaki is essentially a savoury pancake, translated as 'things you like, grilled'. There's meat and stir-fry vegetables, mixed together with a sauce and cooked to a crispy perfection. As an added bonus, we get to flip it ourselves with the spatulas provided. It was good, I was especially fond of the texture, and the zesty carrots were a stark complement to the mild flavour of the shredded cabbage.

Afterwards, we also partake of yakisoba, a stir-fry dish mainly consisting of buckwheat noodles. I enjoy this immensely as well, especially the process of turning over the dish periodically as they cook, before helping myself and threading strands of steaming hot noodles into my mouth. Vik orders a beer, Maggy and I just stick with water. The food is very good, and the staff are all friendly, familiar even. Unsurprising, as Vik had visited quite a few times before. He is also quite comfortable with the young man who serves us, the owner's son, and assures him that the food was 'honto oishii' (very tasty). I cannot fail to realise that Vik's grasp on Japanese is understandably better than mine. He did live here. In addition to studying from a conversational phrase book, I had listened to various chat room conversations off YouTube to get a feel for everyday spoken Japanese. It helped, but only on an intuitive level, and I was far from having any real conversations in Japanese. Vik isn't fluent yet either, and I occasionally pick up on terms he isn't familiar with, but he is in charge of the ordering as I filed away notes for later: in two years, when he returned and we had our fluency contest, I would not be so easily defeated. It may be cheating, but I'm planning to deliberately learn and incorporate uncommon Japanese, just to throw him off.

"Are you full, Thomas?" Maggy checks in on me as I am quiet. It usually prompts some sort of alarm in those I knew, if I stay silent too long. Being introspective is not out of my character, but most people assume that my extrovert side is the dominant one; it's half and half, though I'm not quite sure if I qualify as an ambivert. I nod and indicate that I would like to purchase some alcohol before we head home. Paying our bill, and respects to the owners, we make our way to find the closest Konbinni, which is called Family Mart.

Vik explains that this chain was popular here, along with 7-11 and Lawsons, and as it is my first time inside one, I take great delight in perusing the wares. Another friend of mine, Oliver, had lived in Japan for a year teaching English, similar to what Becky did, and he explained that a lot of single men still didn't know how to cook properly as they were "waiting for wives to do it for them", hence the popularity of instant meals from Konbinnis. The selection isn't cheap take out either, but a wholesome assortment of sandwiches, sushi, riceballs, and ready to microwave noodle/rice dishes, as well as assorted hot foods like chips, fried chicken and local delights. There is even an option to heat your food, for customers who want to consume it right away. Being greeted whenever I walk into a store is also something I'm getting used to: I was taken aback when even the convenience stores treated customers with such attention! It was tempting to get a bunch of potato chips and sweets, out of impulse, but I only end up getting a 750 ml bottle of Sake. I would come to regret it later, but I decide not to get any soda to help with the taste, deciding that I wanted to experience it undiluted while Vik and I talked.

Walking back to their home is another pedestrian wonder. Though they didn't live too far away, the fact that this would be our final trek of the day seems to weigh down my steps, almost as if they are aware the momentum is running out. It is only 9 pm, but that is still over 14 hours since I have been up. Maybe that is why I feel as if I'm being transported to another world, especially once we reach the tunnel. Wind travels through at a different speed to outside, and the sounds of our footsteps add an ethereal overtone. Our voices echo off the walls as we continue to chat about their home, which they warn is small, but homely, so I should feel comfortable. Exiting the tunnel, we trudge up a small slope; I should mention the architecture here was once again different to anything I had seen during the day, though that could just be because it was already dark. We take a left after making it up the slope, and within a couple of metres we arrive at the end of our destination: their flat. Time to unwind from a signature first day.

It is cold indoors, though I expect that it would get warm soon enough. Vik takes a shower while Maggy gives me a tour of the place, and together we unroll my futon mattress, which isn't too thick, but definitely not thin. Once Vik is out of the bathroom, he helps us find the cover and blankets; I would be sleeping at the base of their own mattress tonight. I should mention that they didn't have a bed, which Vik was glad about, as he wanted to experience classic Japanese living conditions. I can only assume that when Maggy moved in (she arrived a few months after he did), she demanded that they get a thicker mattress, and by that logic I deduced that I was sleeping on Vik's old one. Not that I minded, what sane person would?

My friends had given me a grand tour of parts of Tokyo, and now welcomed me into their home, and even provided a bed for me. I wasn't sure how to say it, but I was touched at how they welcomed me so easily, at such short notice. When I told Vik that I needed to see him, and talk face to face, he accepted without further questioning. He truly is my xiong di, a brother that I chose, a man who I would never betray no matter what circumstances we were in.

I jokingly declare that I would be under the sake oath, using alcohol to act as covenant between us to ensure honesty – that applies more to me than him, for while he was a man with little to hide, I am someone comprised of secrets and innumerable interpretations. He takes out a sake set he keeps for occasions such as this, to honour me. Maggy puts on headphones in the next room to give us privacy for our talk.

"Vik xiong di, we are finally together, in a strange land, but far from strangers. I will pour you a toast to show you my esteem. To begin, take your cup into your hand, and I will fill it." I open the bottle I had bought and fill his clay vessel. He takes the bottle once I am done, and does the same for me. The first pour of sake should always be to one's guests, and the guests should receive it with their cup in hand. After that, the rules were more relaxed. We toast each other, arms linked, and drink the sake in one gulp. I fight the urge to wretch, and I snarl silently as the alcohol makes its way down my throat, and into my stomach. Vik makes a face too but we finish our cups.

"Oh yeah, Thomas, I should have warned you, convenience stores aren't known for vintage drinks. Man, this stuff is so rough!"

"It's alright, I don't drink for the taste, though I regret not getting Coke now! You don't have to continue." The taste is on my breath, despite only one cup. I can't put my friend through any more, though I do plan to finish what I had started. He insists on accompanying me.

"I'll drink with you, but I'll use the sake I keep in my fridge!" he ducks out of the room temporarily while I refill my cup. He comes back with a bottle about the same size as mine, but just over half-filled. I drink another cup, and take a moment to recover from my revulsion. I could feel it burning in my stomach, like a fire, or perhaps more accurately described as a glowing coal. Vik is more moderate and sips his cup. He then begins his armour-piercing enquiry,

"Why did you really come here, Thomas? I know you're enjoying yourself, but I can also tell that I'm not the only reason you came." *Sigh...* no point prolonging this any further.

"I'm here... to gain some perspective. Part of that involves you, right here and now, but another part of this trip is Naomi. I have to see her again, because I haven't stopped loving her, not once in the past six years. So, I think, this will help me understand what direction to take next."

"Forgive me, bro, but that's just bullshit." Stunned, I look up directly into the eyes of my best friend. Surely he wasn't already drunk? He continues, eyes locked on to mine,

"You make it out as if seeing her again will solve some great riddle you've struggled with for the last six years. But let's talk about who you've been for the last six years! What kind of direction could she give you that you haven't come to by yourself?"

"Hey! Look, I may be head over heels for her, but I haven't been wasting my life waiting around for her or anything like that! I'm doing what I want, exploring all kinds of different enigmas about the human condition, something that's fascinated me from childhood. I've worked in all kinds of industries to better understand life and living. Seen and experienced so many different things... I'm even considered a mentor to some talented individuals... so surely, that's not nothing?"

"Thomas, I – look, do you remember what happened to you after you broke up with Laura? She was your first girlfriend, and you were so sure of a future together that after she dumped you... you sorta went off the deep end." It was hard to hear this, for I had not really spoken about Laura since I met Naomi all those years ago.

"Come on, Vik, let's not bring Laura into this, okay!? I loved her, emphasis on 'loved', but from what I've heard she's now happily married, a mother, and she's running her family business. Besides, if I'm being honest, Laura and I only stayed together so long because we were each other's first relationship. What I feel for Naomi? It's on a whole different level!"

"Is it? Is it really?!" Vik has a look that desperately seeks to make me understand something, something that should be obvious, except it wasn't to me.

I don't even notice it, but I have gone through several cups of sake at this point, and my head is spinning, slightly. This was unusual, I didn't normally get this way with whiskey, why would sake have this affect? I focus on looking Vik in the eye, determined to defend my stance.

"Yes, it is what I believe. Without having to put in any effort at all, I fell in love with Naomi, and without having to put in any effort, I'm still in love with her. If you weren't my xiong di, I wouldn't even try to explain the way I feel to you. I need your honesty, to hear your opinions, but I don't need to be fixed."

"Look, all I'm saying is that you have a history of getting super self-destructive, dealing with unrequited love. When Laura left you, I was there to help you mend, so I do have some right to mention her, don't I?" I am mollified and soften my tone.

"Yes, yes… I have no secrets from you… but why is this relevant?" He explains himself, and I am seeing something that I might have always known, but denied.

"When your first girlfriend, who you were with for years, decided that she didn't want a future with you, do you recall what happened?" I look away, but I still answer him,

"I… I started to branch out, do different things, got my act together, instead of being such an uxorious boyfriend. So what?" I play it cool, but my voice wobbles, betraying me.

"What does uxorious mean? Never mind, that's not the point, and you know that's a very abridged version of what happened! You swore to never date again and then drove yourself almost to death by working three jobs, and doing a double degree! I watched you lose so much weight, becoming so gaunt and sickly… It hurt, man, especially when you kept getting those nosebleeds! You wouldn't see a doctor or take anything for it, that's how little you cared about what was happening to you! That's what happened to my cheerful, vibrant friend from high school, the same guy who was a role model for others, and always made people feel better by listening to their problems. Don't you see??? You're so used to putting other peoples' happiness above your own that you didn't want to admit how badly you could be hurt!"

"I can admit it now! But I swear, that's all changed, and part of that was because I became friends with Naomi. I still remember every moment of that initial meeting. She was almost like an angel, an angel in a yellow top, denim short skirt, and flip-flops. Meanwhile, there I was, bloodshot and sun burnt from the weekend at my countryside job. Wearing the most horrible clothes I had too, because I didn't have time to do any laundry. That was her first impression of me! God, it makes me cringe to this day… But I changed after we became friends, you know? Starting eating better, gave up unreasonable shifts, and even starting proper hygiene again. In fact, when Naomi joked about how my hair was greasy, I started to condition it, and started wearing nicer clothes too. And I still like getting lots of attention from girls, doesn't that mean I'm moving on?"

"No. No it doesn't. You get attention from other girls, but not from HER. And that's my whole point! Everything you did to impress her only made you seem weirder, and you know I love you but, for the love of God, you have to let the crazy out a little bit at a time, man!" Vik wasn't shouting, but he was emphasising each syllable slowly, as if to get it through my skull. I drink another cup, cursing the taste. The bottle still had a third of that foul substance left. I was feeling hollow and burnt out.

"So what, huh? So what if she doesn't feel the same way? Even if she doesn't want to date me, she's an awesome person! Even if it's just as friends, I'm glad to have known her, I admire her in the same way I admire you, my xiong di! Look at you, living away from home, making progress through your career with a wonderful woman by your side?

I'm not even jealous, that's how much I care about you and Maggy!"

"Thanks, Thomas!" We are surprised by Maggy, who communicates from the room next door, indicating that if she could hear us through the screen, the neighbours probably could too. The content didn't matter, they most likely didn't have a sufficient grasp on English to understand us, but noise was a problem all the same. Vik had told me stories about the non-confrontational nature of people here, and he had previously received polite notes asking him to keep it down. The Japanese do love their quietness I suppose. Suddenly self-conscious, I lower my voice to ask him,

"Do you have something to help wash out this taste? I'll take anything." He proceeds to get me a carton of grapefruit juice from the fridge. The drink tried its best, but I could barely taste anything after the sake. Vik continues where we left off,

"I'm flattered, as the praise comes from a very smart and capable man. But ask yourself, what kind of life do you lead nowadays? Why do you think your parents are trying to get you to marry? It's because your life is aimless! Don't deny it, Thomas. You apply for jobs that are beneath you, refusing to get paid for any of those seminars or private teaching, even refusing offers to do regular speeches... is it because you still don't believe in material wealth? And no girl can live up to the impossible standards you've set, because to qualify – to even stand a chance, they'd have to be Naomi. It's not fair on anyone involved, and in the end, you'd rather not have any intimacy with another girl, that's the impression I get from you." He pauses as his words sink in, and continues,

"You have real potential, real talent, but instead I see you wasting it because deep down you don't want to move forward with your life. Other people see you as this almost invulnerable, inhuman being, but I know you as the kid from high school who shared his books with me when I started my first day – no one else offered. You're hurting bro, even if you say otherwise, and it's hurting me to see you like this, after all this time." I look down, a little ashamed by his pleading, but I refuse to be cowed for long.

"Are you asking me to do better for you? You've never understood how much I have to sacrifice to keep the peace… Am I selfish to hold on to my feelings? You know, just once, I want to do something selfish without having to feel guilty about it!"

"You've never seemed to understand, Thomas, that I want you to do better for YOU! I accept you unconditionally, I want you to know that you're worth it!"

"I acknowledge your love! Here, I drink you another toast!" And I drain the remainder of the bottle, struggling afterwards to hold it together, to keep everything inside. I understood now what had happened – the emotional imbalance caused by this conversation had sapped my internal strength, and without those convictions I was a sitting duck for the alcohol. I wasn't actually drunk, but I was definitely out of my element, unsure how my normally controlled body would react. Vik seems mildly impressed, and returns the gesture.

"I toast you, my brother from another mother!" He also drains his bottle. It was a milestone for us, we never drank together back home, as I usually abstained, but tonight we drank more sake than we had ever tried in our lives. I am touched by this realisation, and I let down my walls slightly,

"The truth is… I came to Japan, to say goodbye, to you and Naomi, just in case I do decide to enter a secluded priesthood somewhere. I'm choosing to do it now, because I can feel my mortality, xiong di – I'm losing more hair every day, and my eyesight is starting to get worse, so I just wanted… I just wanted to see you both, and be remembered as a young man… Do you think our bond can survive that? I have to see Naomi again. I mean, I'm in Japan, how could I not? And when I see her, and tell her how I feel – that I love her… I'll make my peace with everything. This chapter of my life is about to close, so I wanted to give the ending a j – to do it justice – uh oh… *Errrrughyp.*"

My body had decided that it couldn't suppress the alcohol any longer and would simply jettison it. In three consecutive waves, I unleash the contents of dinner onto my host's rug and table. To my shame, Vik has to help me to the shower to clean up, and he finds a spare set of clothes for me to change into, the ones I normally used for sleeping. Miserably, I kneel in the shower, letting the hot water wash over my body, trying to remove the stain of shame that hung over me as I rinse the stain of vomit off my clothes. I suppose Becky was right, you do learn more about yourself when you purge, and I continue to expel several smaller loads down bathroom drain. As it washed away, I feel my head spinning less, and I decide to get out before I waste any more of their hot water.

Bashfully, I poke my head back into the room where my crime took place. They had done a remarkable job at removing the evidence, the only tell-tale sign being a stain on the previously all white rug. But the two, kindly and concerned, usher me in, and do not berate me in the slightest. They give me water to drink, and tuck my trembling self into bed, where I quickly drift off into a dreamless sleep. I feel… less alone? That is my final thought before giving in to complete oblivion.

Chapter 8

I awaken, unsure what time it is, but not hung over, I think: I didn't have a headache, I can see normally and suffer no loss of equilibrium when I try to stand up. Vik is already up in the next room, so I join him.

"*Ohayo* (Good morning)," I whisper, so as to not wake Maggy. He asks me how I'm doing, and once assured that I am fine, he explains that he is heading out to give a lecture at the university. It is only 7 am, but he is due there at 9, so is heading out for breakfast and the bus stop. I accompany him, deciding that I can easily retrace my steps back to their home, and Vik gives me the keycard that will allow me entrance if Maggy is still asleep. He informs me that Maggy had taken a sick day in order to make sure I'm alright. I feel bad, I have inconvenienced my hosts, but Vik explains that after the night we had, Maggy would appreciate some time to recharge too.

We make our way back through the tunnel that lost none of the charm from last night. At this hour, there were even schoolchildren making their way to various institutes, and a lot more road traffic too. In the open, we can use our normal volume to speak, which seems to bring me back from my alternate state of consciousness. I feel pretty normal. Soon we cross the tracks and are outside Zushi Station. Vik has to wait for a bus, but in the 30 minutes before it arrives we will have breakfast. Or, he eats breakfast, while I only have a black tea, not trusting my stomach with solids just yet. Between bites of his eggs and toast, he continues last night's discussion.

"So what are you going to do? Marriage is a big deal, but are you seriously able to give up secular life?" I shrug and respond.

"No meat, no wine, no women. I spend all day reading, writing, doing simple chores to strengthen my character, and pursuing self-cultivation. Not the worst life imaginable."

"Yeah, but I dunno, it seems like a waste with your personality. At least you won't molest any kids, right?"

"All things worth doing require some kind of sacrifice. Isn't that the law of equivalent exchange?"

"Hah that's pretty dark man! I remember *Full Metal Alchemist*, though I don't watch much anime anymore. No time! But anyway, let's say you do get married, what do you do then?"

"Well, I would need to get a regular job, or win the lottery. I live just fine right now, but I don't think it's appropriate for my wife, or any kids we have. Regardless of what I do, I will be a responsible and dutiful husband, and ensure she is treated with every comfort I can afford." If I do get married, I would have to make sure my wife is looked after properly. But there is always the chance that she wouldn't care for me, and I would be off the hook, at least until mother found another candidate. I decide to leave it for now, it is something to worry about after I left Japan and returned home. Vik resumes his line of questioning,

"What about love? Could you love her while still loving Naomi?"

"I don't see what love has to do with this. It's marriage, and one arranged too. A partnership that will only work if both people are prepared to work for it, regardless of how they feel. My parents made theirs work for a long time after they fell out of love, if only because of the kids. So yeah, as long as she isn't a psycho bitch, I think I could grow in love, even if I don't fall for her."

"Man, sometimes I am reminded that we come from very different worlds! You've always been hung up on duty and honour to family."

"Hah! And you've always been fond of spouting dangerous new-age ideas that could threaten social collapse! Individuality? Freedom of expression? What about the greater good!?" I am being playful now, as I usually am.

"There can't be a greater good if there isn't lesser good my friend." Vik does make a valid point, but I supersede his reasoning,

"Lesser goods work in the short term; they don't guarantee a better future. Not in the way being future oriented can."

"There's still no guarantee though!"

"No, there are no guarantees in life, but I feel more comfortable knowing that I tried to make a difference, in a way I can justify."

We are sobered by our different stances, but laugh it off, and decide to end the little debate. Vik's bus makes its way to the terminal now anyway. We leave the diner, and embrace each other, maybe for the last time.

"Don't you dare disappear on me, Thomas!" he jokingly threatens. Unfazed, I simply state,

"I've said my goodbyes to you, just in case I do. I can't promise anything at this point, xiong di."

"Man, you are so annoying, I should poke you in the eyes!" We both laugh at the false venom in his tone, knowing that it could be the last time we banter like this in person. He gets on the bus, as I stand and watch him disappear from view. It was now time to get to work! I had to redeem myself after last night's fiasco.

I head to the Family Mart, which seems much closer in the daylight. Vik had told me that some of my mess remained on the rug, which I am determined to clean up. I find a whole pack of antibacterial wipes to aid me on my redemption. I also pick up some eggs and bread, which I admit took longer than I would have liked. In Japan, the eggs are white shelled, and the bread is not like large western loaves, but smaller and sliced thicker. That made it hard for me to immediately locate them in the store. I also pick up a bottle of coke to help me recover from the sake, and a bag of chips, because I like potato chips and God knows I need them now. It was easy enough to make my way back to their home from there, and upon entering the kitchen/dining room, I see that Margaret is indeed awake, having just finished breakfast. I smile as cheerfully as I can,

"Hey, Maggy, I hope my snoring didn't keep you up!" Returning my smile, she reassures me, and nods her thanks as I hand her the bread and eggs. She commends me on my thoughtfulness, but I confess that Vik had told me they were running low, which is why I decided to get some more. We laugh and the mild awkwardness evaporates. Wasting no further time, I help to pack up the spare futon, while she helps me plan my next destination. On my knees, I begin thoroughly combing through the rug, occasionally curious at the undigested food bits I found, namely carrot and cabbage. I guess I should chew for longer in future? Once the solids had been removed, I begin to repeatedly go over the general area with my sanitary wipes; I have worked as a cleaner before, both in the domestic and public sectors, so I'm not afraid of getting my hands dirty. There's always a sense of satisfaction in leaving a place better than you found it, and I know enough about different types of cleaning to handle most contaminations. In this case, I want to remove the solid particles, preventing any chance that I would rub them into surface, and then apply the wipes in different directions, depending on the grain of the rug. It isn't a perfect job, as I'm working without my usual gear, but fortunately there wasn't any odour to worry about on this occasion.

I finish cleaning to the best of my ability, though still feel unsatisfied. They might decide to burn that rug, once I left. I sit down to a glass of coke and pop open my potato chips. Maggy shows me the laptop, with my path laid out on Google Maps.

"Thanks, Thomas, it looks good as new. Here's the directions to Fujiyama. I'm pretty jealous, you're staying at the Mt Fuji Premium Resort, on the mountain base!"

"I know! The tour guide got me a nice last-minute deal. I think I'll try to sneak up the mountain, as the pathways are closed around this time of year. Too many deaths apparently. Not that I have anything to worry about, I'm immortal!" Maggy smiles, humouring my antics.

"Just look after yourself, okay? You know that Vik and I worry about you. There's a lot of people who would be sad if something happened to you." I have the good grace to not spoil her sincerity with any flippant remarks. She really is a wonderful person, like a sister to me. I finish my drink, wash the glass, and collect my gear: packing did not take long. We head to the door, and share a quick hug.

"I'd better go, I'm already behind schedule. Thanks for everything, Maggy. I love you." She pats me on the back.

"Yeah, yeah, me too." We laugh and part ways. She collects the mail, while I wave farewell and continue my journey.

I'm not going to lie, I had been completely relying on my friends for public transportation cues ever since I arrived, and without them I was spending much longer between stations, and bus terminals. Thankfully, I was capable of asking for directions, and the transportation officers knew enough English to guide me on my way. Five hours later, my behind was sore from the buses and trains, but I had made it to Kawaguchiko Station, the closest to Mt Fuji. It's breath taking to observe the landscape, so many mountainous ranges! It would probably be something the locals are used to, but I came from a less topographic place, so the wonder of seeing mountains reminded me of Bilbo Baggins, specifically his longing for them in Tolkien's *The Lord of the Rings*.

I wander around the bus terminal, which is really more a parking lot with bus shelters. The Fuji Premium Resort, like most hotels in the area, offers a free shuttle bus to their establishment. It wasn't due for another 20 minutes though, so I float through the tourist centre and the transport station. Kawaguchiko Station is located at a town, but my resort is isolated further up at the mountain base, surrounded by woodlands. Supposedly there are deer here, but not bears, which used to be here long but now are only found up north in areas like Hokkaido. I entertain the notion of meeting a bear in Japan, but decide that it wasn't worth it – what if my jacket got damaged?

The time passes quickly enough, though two other shuttle buses had arrived from different hotels, and those false starts almost caused me to miss my actual shuttle due to resigned indifference. Fortunately, the driver calls me by name, and along with three other passengers already inside, we make our way to the resort. While I'm the only one waiting at this depot, this shuttle service has three other stops prior; as I was the last one, we are all grateful to be able to reach our destination soon.

Driving regulations in Japan are curious, I couldn't decipher how they interpreted certain signals or even lights. The roads are small, maybe only slightly larger than a single lane from home, but everyone is efficient and managed to easily transverse them. Every time I saw oncoming traffic, I had an instinctual, fearful flash of a sideward collision, but the mathematical principle of parallel lines held, and I soon grew accustomed to it.

We arrive a little after 5 pm, and the check-in is a smooth transition. The resort is not a typical hotel, more like a villa. All the guest rooms are located on the 2nd floor in the same multi-storey building. Ground floor is reception and the gift shop, filled with typical knick-knacks and specialty items exclusive to Mt Fuji. One floor below is a basement filled with an anime library and games room/arcade, which would have been nice if I could read Japanese or enjoyed video games. Levels 3 and 4 are the 'Top of the Forest' buffet restaurants, dinner and breakfast respectively. There is a sports facility next door, and an onsen, or hot spring, located about five minutes' walk away. I get settled in my room, which unsurprisingly has a vending machine located just outside. I swear, I'm going to miss seeing them when I return home.

I return to the receptionist, who informs me that dinner would be on in an hour, and that I could access their laundry at the building adjacent. I'm wearing my black tracksuit underneath my trench coat, which I had fortunately taken off before drinking with Vik last night. The laundry room is easy to find, and the lone security guard patrolling the corridors of that building indicates it is a 24-hour facility. As I proceed to use their laundromat, I ready myself for the smell. My clothes from the previous night were very damp, but aside from that, they weren't smelly at all! To add to my good fortune, I discover that laundry powder is provided free of charge, and the washer and dryer only cost 200 and 100 yen respectively. Amazing value, and the machines looked quite new too!

Once that is settled, I realise that the next hour and a half would be spent here, so I explore my immediate surroundings. Would you believe it, there is a small arcade in this block as well, and I spend the next 30 minutes blowing 1,000 yen on the claw skill tester. As a fisherman might say, I almost caught a huge one, but I let it go last minute. Translation: I did not catch anything. Eventually, my laundry is complete, and I make my way back to my room, before heading up to floor 3 for dinner. It cost 5,000 yen, but I suppose a premium buffet would be about that much. It's not like there were any other restaurants here, though the resort did offer take-out pizza for guests who wanted something other than a buffet.

I am greeted the moment I walk out of the elevator, and the young lady asks for my room number to send the bill. Then I am seated in an exquisitely furnished dining lounge. There is an immediate ambience about this place, as I begin to relax and take in my surroundings. Beautiful dining music plays softly overhead, while the dimly lit tabled areas give a gentle impression of privacy, almost as if to say that each guest is special here, that there was no need to rush the meal. It seemed to whisper *Enjoy yourself, however you please.* I help myself to ice water, and a glass of chilled oolong tea, before strolling through the buffet selections. I'm not sure if they had done so deliberately, but the colour coordination of the various dishes made for an attractive, and appetising, display. This buffet was a combination of Japanese/Chinese inspired meals, some Mediterranean dishes, and an assortment of a salad options. I start with a platter of rice, tempura fish, teriyaki stir-fry vegetables, and miso soup. Once I'm finished with that, I help myself to baked potato and macaroni, both cooked in at least three different types of cheese, yet it isn't heavy at all! The restaurant also gives complimentary crab legs, each practically the size of a child's arm, as well as a platter of medium rare, chilled beef slices, and wedges that come with a delicately spiced aioli/gorgonzola dip. I enjoyed the beef and potato wedges, but avoid the crab legs, as I have a mild shellfish allergy I did not want to trigger this evening. My final platter consists of plain white rice and soup to balance out the richness of what I had consumed. Ah, if only I could take Vik and Maggy here, they would have enjoyed this immensely, being partial to fine food, and of course my good company. Well, when I'm not throwing up on their furniture.

I sit for a moment, to digest both food and thoughts for tomorrow. It's my intention to wander through the woods, until I arrive closer to the base. Mt Fuji is normally traversed from one of the lower mountain ridges, which one could reach by taking a bus to 'Mt Fuji Subaru Line 5th Station'. Quite a mouthful, but maybe in Japanese it rolls off the tongue more smoothly. The trek is an established one, and even had several rest points where mountaineers could purchase oxygen tanks and other supplies. However, such established pathways to the mountaintop are closed during this season, especially with the recent snowfall. This did not deter me; I've gone skiing before, back in my home country, and I had already experienced the snow version of being thrown into the deep end. Tonight I am feeling quite nostalgic, which the ambience and food may have greatly contributed to.

On the second day of that holiday, I grew ambitious, and armed with only a basic lesson, I tried one of the more difficult slopes. The result was a spectacular failure, as I lost control almost immediately, falling over at such speeds that my skis were wrenched from my feet, and I proceeded to roughly tumble for several hundred meters before slowing down, eventually stopping. For a moment, I lay still and face down in the snow, before springing back to life. Taking a sudden, long breath, followed by subsequent deep breaths, I picked myself out from the snow. I was shaking, adrenaline coursing through my system, but otherwise unharmed, and mostly glad I decided to do this unaccompanied. Naomi and Louise were on this trip as well, along with some other friends, and needless to say my pride could be injured more easily than my body would be if I made a fool of myself. Especially in front of Naomi, who, truth be told, was the main reason I decided to come here in the first place. I then trekked back up the slope, while gasping to breathe due to the altitude, and was lucky to recover most of my gear. Sadly, however, I only ever found one of my gloves. Is it not saddening to think that a pair was now separated forever? I still have that one glove, though stopped wearing any afterwards, having discovered that my circulation was good enough to handle the sub-zero temperatures. The good news was that the confronting experience gave me a lot more confidence, hence why my skiing abilities improved dramatically afterwards.

Still, I will not be skiing on Mt Fuji on this trip, I will simply scale it with sheer force of will! I take a break from my mental trepidations, and decide to enjoy dessert before the place packs everything away for the night. I chose some fresh fruit, grapes in particular, and a cup of layered cheesecake. A few cakes beckoned, but I'm full now, and only partake of one cube, a caramel with cream. Along with some hot tea, it is the idyllic way to end a sumptuous dinner. I know that I can sleep well tonight, but before that, there is one more feature to try: the onsen. After a long day, a hot springs soak would be welcome.

I make my way downstairs and see the friendly concierge woman from before. After asking about the onsen, she tells me it is 1,000 yen per session, which I consider a bargain. As I'm walking away, however, she motions for me to return, and says that as the onsen closed in an hour she would give me an extra voucher to use tomorrow, free of charge. Touched by her generosity, I bow my thanks, and try to navigate my way to the lodge that housed the onsen. It is not too far away, and though the pathways has some confusing twists (in the dark anyway), the signs are sufficient to get me there. I punch in the numbers on my voucher, and the door slides open, to be greeted by an elderly woman. She explains that the men's section is to my left, as mixed bathing is not allowed at this particular onsen. I make my way to a wood-lined changing room, equipped with a bathroom and several lockers to house our clothes.

Nudity is required, which I had not been aware of, but I am already here so why not? It is a little nerve wracking, however, as there are three other people also going in, two elderly and one about my age. I strip down, a little hesitantly at first, as I had not been naked with anyone for a long time; Vik has a key to my house and before he left the country, he would often drop by unannounced, hence close calls on several occasions, but that was it. Seeing how boldly the old men walked about, I decided to just engage in the moment, finding my zen, and was soon able to ease myself into the quiet rhythm of the place. At least it was warm here: shrinkage is not flattering for any guy. While I strip down to my underwear, I see my reflection, and despite sounding vain, I liked what the active locomotion in Japan had done for me.

As I mentioned to Vik earlier, I had been intensely working out in the week before I arrived, telling myself that it was to get in shape for the travelling. I saw clearly shaped muscles along my pectorals, something that enhanced my broad frame, and true to my word I did have a basic six-pack, though I found that the diet here had added extra definition to them. There's a surprising lack of fat in the food here, even with fried dishes! Feeling more confident, I finish undressing and head to the showering stations opposite the large rectangular tub. The correct procedure is to sit or kneel, and thoroughly use soaps or shampoos to rinse any impurities off the body. I enjoy the lather, as they had provided products containing sesame oil for hair and royal jelly in the body cleansers. I almost forgot that I am here to use a hot spring, so pleasant is the shower.

Once finished, I climb into the tub, taking care not to let my little cloth mix with the water, as it is considered improper. Instead, I fold it into a small rectangle and place it on my head. I recall Jake had mentioned that there was usually a screen of Mt Fuji in many onsen in Japan, but all this place has are tall glass windowpanes, and a door that leads outside. As we were at the base of Mt Fuji, maybe it was a statement? If that was the case, I really appreciate how subtle the Japanese could be! I soak for a while, trying to meditate. In my zen state, I try to compose a poem that reflects my journey so far.

An atheist tries to believe in God,

A flower with thorns, waiting to be picked.

Confusion reflects the sleeping mind,

Still waters reflect the truest self.

Where to find, forgotten treasure lost,

Preserved amidst the winter frost?

I open my eyes, aware that I have zoned out, maybe for 20 minutes, and am now quite overcooked. I make my way out, slowly, my body extra sensitive and woozy from the heat I'm emanating. I am no longer feeling cooked, merely dizzy. A water dispenser helps me rehydrate, as I drink several cups in quick succession. Feeling my strength return, I breathe deeply, and feel it travelling through my body, reorienting me. All the rest of the patrons had left, and as I make my way out, I see the old lady at the counter is absent, probably taking care of the women's section. I walk out into the darkness, the cool air a refreshing change of temperature. Somehow, in my dazed state, I return to my room, collapse into bed and immediately drift into a dreamless sleep.

Chapter 9

I think I went to bed at about 11 pm, and when I awaken, the blinds prevent me from immediately knowing what time it is. Checking my phone, I see that it is 6:12 am, and I am happy to be up at this time, for I wanted to see the sunrise. Putting on my long black jacket, I set off to explore the grounds. There is some light already, but the true sunrise is due in about 15 minutes, so I want to be fully awake when those rays cast themselves over the resort. A few people are already up, mostly a Chinese team of students who are wearing red parka jackets. Pretty soon, the full majesty of solar radiation illuminates this area, perhaps enhanced by the white, reflective snow. I am watching the sun rise, in the land of the rising sun!

It's not breakfast time until another hour, so I amuse myself in the basement arcade. I put in 100 yen in a pachinko machine, though it is a virtual one without those charming metal balls falling through the pins. I am unable to read the instructions so just start pushing buttons and twisting the knob at random intervals, basically whenever the screen starts flashing more lights and sounds. It quickly becomes dull, as I could not follow the storyline (yes, the game had a storyline incorporating pachinko as some form of space battle) but then I am delighted as the entire machine begins flashing, and I see that my credits have changed. I had originally put in 100 yen, which gave me 100 shots, and on the 26th, I had apparently hit a jackpot. The numbers kept climbing higher and higher, until they reach over 2000, at which point I press random buttons to try and collect my prize. No money falls out, but I do receive a bronze token with 777 on it. I am done with the game now, despite having

56 credits left, and take my token upstairs. The staff at reception aren't sure what the token is for, and one accompanies me back downstairs to read the instructions. He determines that it is a token for more points. I decide to keep it, as a lucky charm, rather than cash it in or continue playing. It is breakfast time anyway, and I'm in good spirits.

Did you know why this place is called the Fuji Premium Resort? You can see the mountaintop up close, especially on the highest floor, where breakfast is conducted. I am equally impressed at the spread as it is not only delightfully varied but also arranged with the most appealing aesthetics in mind. Colourful too. I see little square slices of bread in green, black, and white; they are green tea, charcoal, and normal bread flavoured respectively. And a platter of croissants too, which I could not resist taking four or five at once (they were mini croissants, the size of my palm). Of course, in keeping with the theme of local cuisine, I also help myself to rice porridge, which I eat with dried seafood flakes and wakame seaweed. How hearty this breakfast was, especially after I discovered the tray of potato nuggets! I am in good spirits, and have a decent appetite despite last night's feast. I would need it as if I wanted to make it to the mountaintop, but I am careful to not over eat, as I didn't want to worry about a bathroom break on the way there or back. Well, maybe just another platter of croissants and juice, surely that would be fine.

I am still wearing my tracksuit, which I had brought along specifically to climb Mt Fuji. I decide to not take my jacket or scarf; the lighter I travelled the better. In fact, I only take my phone, my room keycard, and a small glass vial, all fitting easily in my side pocket. It's 10:30 am now, and I head out past the complex to scale this famous mountain.

It begin simply enough, as I make my way into the forest, away from the resort. The forests look as if they begin to clear, but I know that it is a deceptive openness. With sufficient snowfall, the trees are buried, and I'm actually making my way on top of the branches right now. It is tricky, but I manage to work out a system of testing my weight as I tread towards the mountain. The view is breath taking, and not only because the physical efforts make it harder to breathe. Even as I'm accustoming my breathing patterns to these conditions, I can't fail to marvel at the sights. Once I reach a bit farther up, the trees begin to reappear more densely, and my footing becomes relatively surer.

Navigation is less of a problem as my idea is to make it directly up the mountain as much as possible. Despite being no mountaineer I'm determined, and whenever relevant, I simply scale the less difficult terrain to go directly up, rather than making my way up in a zig-zag weave. It is tiring, and soon I have to rely more and more on the paths of least resistance. Gravity is a stubborn mistress. Occasionally, I slip as I make my way higher, and most of the bruising I've currently sustained is from losing my footing. One time I had to try to brace myself against a ledge, and ended up scraping my knee on a branch hidden just beneath the snow. As I encounter the rockier parts of the mountains, I regret not having some form of gloves, although in general I prefer the sensitivity that my uncovered fingers offered.

Despite all the discomforts, I am enjoying myself. The air, the smells, and even the light are different here, cleaner and spiritually uplifting. To be honest, the main reason I wanted to make it to the top was to see things from her perspective. Naomi had been there at the peak, and although I doubt I could identify the exact spot in her photo, I want to experience standing in her position, as if it would give me insight into her mind. Maybe it's my way of compensating for the distance between us; how strange that despite being physically closer to her than I had been in years (yet still so far away), this mountain was reminding me, more than ever, of the uncertainty which obscured my true feelings. I'm in love with her, had stayed in love all this time. Often, I think that perhaps what I'm doing was unhealthy, that maybe I'm addicted to the idea of loving someone unobtainable. 'Courtly Love', as it is known in classic literature. Yet what I said to Vik was true! We definitely qualify as real friends, in spite, or maybe because, of how I feel. We are people who could express honest opinions to each other (with the exception of my feelings), and who had shared experiences. I enjoyed it when I made her laugh or learned more about who she was, and genuinely cared about each other's wellbeing. Yes, she was very attractive, but she was also adventurous, kind, refined and determined, with a work ethic second to none, and a zest for life that was infectious. I do not think it is surprising to fall in love with such a person. I want to think I am a better man for having known her.

What did she think when she witnessed the sky and the realm beneath her that day? I can only guess, for my phone beeps. It is about 4 pm, I have been on my side adventure for over five hours. My phone had been fully charged when I left in the morning, but the cold, along with the stupid fact that my GPS had been left on, resulted in only 15% of battery remaining. 14%, it is fading fast. According to the app, I had about a quarter of the mountain left before I hit the approximate peak, but I also know that I'm not in a direct path to my hotel, and being stranded on a mountain that was supposed to be off limits did not appeal to me. I know that my journey could not go any further, unless I entertain suicide by exposure, which I do not. Resignedly, I take out the tiny empty glass bottle, and fill it with the whitest patch of snow I can find. I wanted to take snow/water from the peak back with me as a souvenir, but this would have to suffice. I do what I can to reduce battery drain from my phone, and periodically turn the GPS on and off to check my position as I return to the hotel, slightly dejected but also kind of glad I'm being responsible. By my standards anyway.

The time is 7:26 pm, and I see the outline of the resort in the dark, the lights are twinkling, beckoning me back after a long day. I am too tired for a buffet dinner, but that's alright, I need a change of pace. When I get to the reception, it is closer to 9 pm. A man with glasses, the same one who helped me with pachinko earlier in the day, assists me in ordering a pizza, I choose basic margarita for 2,000 yen, and head to my room to shower before it arrives.

I am exhausted, mentally as well as physically. Soon after I step out of the bathroom, refreshed from my shower, there's a knock on my door – the pizza has arrived. I nod my thanks to the girl who delivers it. It smells good, with a sharp aroma of cheese, probably parmesan. After wolfing down a few bites, I am aware of my thirst and quickly go outside to the vending machine. One coke isn't enough, so I grab a lemonade as well. My trek was more challenging than I had imagined, as I sip my drink and observe myself in the mirror. Quite a bit of bruising covers one side now, all of which was covered by the bathrobe provided by the hotel. It is why the delivery girl didn't seem too alarmed, though I suppose they would respect my privacy here and not ask questions, even if I answered the door looking like I had been in a car crash. Most of the blood around my right thigh and knees had been washed away from the shower, and the superficial wounds would dry soon. Hands were scraped, but not too badly.

My phone and tracksuit are actually still in one piece, and I am grateful that my fondness of black clothing camouflaged the dried blood. I reflect about what had happened since I left for my climb, and consider what I could have done differently if I were to try again. Before long I can feel my eyelids getting heavy, and I settle into bed, my spirit faintly bitter about the disappointment. I was at Fuji, and I had failed to reach the peak. Maybe I was ashamed of my cowardice, for I felt relief when my phone gave me a reason to come back down. Or it could be that I felt cheated at not being able to reach the peak. Whatever it was, I soon stop thinking about it as I close my eyes and feel my mind dimming.

Chapter 10

Initially greeted by a stiff and sore body, I stay in bed past the allotted breakfast time. I am not hungry, so do not mind, but I'm surprised at a piece of good fortune: the bruised swellings from yesterday had gone down overnight, and while still sporting patches of discolouration, I feel fine. After rousing myself out of bed and doing a quick physical, I check my recharged phone and learn it is about 10 am. Check out was in an hour, and as I had little packing to do, I simply put on my normal attire and pass the time in the gift shop downstairs. The check-out procedure is simple, and mainly concerned with any unpaid bills: for me it is a breakfast and dinner buffet, plus last night's pizza, which in total amounted to 8,000 yen. I understand now that while the room wasn't especially expensive, staying multiple nights with multiple buffets could quickly become so. Thank you, Fuji Premium Resort, you certainly lived up to your name.

The shuttle bus arrives at 11:00 am, and I find that it is full of other passengers too. The term 'shuttle bus' is a bit of a misnomer, for it is more a van, and on this instance there is a young lady who has given me a very charming smile. I smile back, quite charmed, and am about to attempt conversation with my paltry Japanese (though I suppose she may have been Chinese). Timing is not on my side however, as a whole of team of red jackets suddenly make their way from inside the building and begin to board the vehicle. The moment is swept away, and becomes part of the realm of what could have been. Once we reach Kawaguchiko Station, everyone except the girl disembarks, and I suppose that if we did have anything to say to each other, it would have to wait until our paths crossed again, unlikely as that may be. At

Kawaguchiko, I purchase a bus ticket to Mishima, where after three hours, I would be riding the train again. Not just any train, but a Shinkansen bullet train, the fastest rail in Japan. It would take me to Shizuoka Station, where I could rendezvous with Jake.

I make it to Mishima by early mid-afternoon, and am excited to see it lightly snowing! The JR office has a small queue, but I am processed quickly enough and get myself a reserved seat on the next Shinkansen to Shizuoka, which would be arriving in just over 10 minutes. This is my first time riding a bullet, and I'm curious as to what is in store. I'm not expecting the Concorde, but it goes without saying that it has to be fast! As I bide time on the platform, I see a little kiosk, selling not only food but all manner of news agency wares too. Did I mention that the Japanese are so organised, even their trash is separated into different categories? I am used to 'waste' and 'recycling' where I'm from, but here, I'm paying extra attention to where I dispose of 'paper/cardboard', food waste', 'metals' and 'other waste': this is a country which prides itself on thoroughness!

I prepare to board the now approaching train, and can distinguish it immediately. It is sleek looking, and I'm mildly impressed at a particular design feature that muffled the displaced air as it came to a stop. The inside reminds me of a more spacious airplane's, with lanes that feature overhead space for luggage storage, and even a few passengers in deep sleep. A bathroom is located on one of the carriages (I was in compartment three). I settle into a comfortable chair, by public transport standards anyway, and before long, we are bound for Shizuoka. In mere seconds, I can feel the momentum as the train kicks off, and while it is not exactly unpleasant, I'm glad to have an empty stomach.

After arriving in good time, and mentally noting that in future I must take advantage of the Shinkansen more often. I decide that it is time for lunch, and I know just the place: McDonald's! I take a picture of the place once the Google Maps leads me here, and proceed to order. This place did not have an English menu, but they have an illustrated one which I was able to point to, trying to be as polite as possible. Having been to many McDonald's in my time, this was nonetheless my first one in Japan. The fillet-o-fish burger ordered was good, but I am in love with the fries, which came super-sized! All in all, pretty decent, and as the meal only cost about 600 yen, I'm tempted to order more, but ultimately decide against it. It is time to head to my destination, a flat that Jake is staying in while he trained here.

Walking there takes some time, maybe 40 minutes (according to my phone), but the air is good and I take interest with the change in architecture. This place holds a different appeal to Tokyo, less advertising, almost unassumingly inviting. Before I know it, I'm already there, and knock on the door. After a bit of fumbling, Jake opens it to greet me, coughing, with an ashen face and slumped posture. What had happened to him?!

"Woah, you don't look too good, let's shut this door!" We make our way inside, and head to his room, where he collapses on the bed. He has an actual bed, not a futon, but I suppose his family wanted him to be as comfortable as possible while staying here. I quickly check his forehead then pulse, feeling that the beat was rapid and weakened, not good news. He has a slight temperature, his complexion is pale, and his breathing is raspy. He quietly explains that his throat is sore too. Tokyo had given him a chill, and he has been recovering since yesterday. We had not been in much contact since the day we parted ways at the train station, but he tells me that his symptoms have only worsened yesterday. When I ask him if he has any taken any medicines, he mentions that all he could find at the convenience store are lozenges, and I see a half-empty pack lying on the bedside desk. Of course, I think to myself, over the counter pain-relief medicines aren't as readily available in Japan, even at pharmacies. He begins to grow distressed, as he explains to me that his initial training session is in seven hours. His voice, so flat and dejected, continues to berate his situation,

"I'm weak. That's what they're going to think. And they're right… I came all the way to Japan, and I get sick the moment I arrive…" His self-criticisms are interrupted as he get ups, clears his throat, and spits out some mucus. He then drops back into bed, and shivers, exhausted by the effort it takes to walk to his bathroom. I try to reassure him.

"You're being too hard on yourself, getting ill is to be expected if you are exposed to cold conditions. Plus, you're a thin guy, less insulation. They'll be other training sessions once you're better…"

It breaks my heart to see the look of anguish on his face, and his eyes grow misty. His voice is now thick with emotion, not just mucus lining the walls of his throat.

"Tonight the head instructor, Washizu-sensei, is coming to welcome us personally. He won't be back for another month, and this will be his first impression of me! But I can't train like this, I can barely stand. I'm sorry, you came here for nothing, I've let you down too, Thomas, after getting you to help me write an introduction letter."

As I try to reassure him that he has done no such thing, I wonder about what introduction letter? Getting up, I go to boil water, and prepare some tea. At the Fuji Premium Resort, guests had been given free samples of green tea, and at the risk of sounding cheap, I had grabbed more than a few packets before leaving. It was coming in handy now, as I prepare a cup, and blow, eventually cooling it enough for Jake to drink. He does so slowly but finishes the cup. Then I remember, months back Jake had emailed me if I knew anyone who could help him translate a letter into Japanese, which I had passed along to Naomi. I didn't read the letter, so I didn't immediately realise it was for this trip. Recalling this, and hearing his disappointment, made me think of Naomi, and how I regretted not making a better impression when we first met. I decide on a course of action.

"Jake, where are the door keys?"

"Uh… on the kitchen table, why?"

"You're going to make it there tonight, with some luck, but I am going to find some things before we can make that happen."

Taking the keys, I head out and check my phone. The closest yakkyoku, or chemist, is barely 10 minutes away. I immediately head there, but outside I wonder if it is actually a pharmacy (it was a small room, without aisles of products like I am used to seeing). The staff, one young and one middle-aged, greet me in the manner I have grown accustomed to here, and I try to confirm if this was the place.

"Konichiwa, kore wa yakkyoku desuka (Hello, is this the pharmacy)?" They quickly assure me that it is. I steady myself for the next part.

"Watashi no tomodachi wa kibun ga yokuarimasen. Anata wa itamidome (My friend sick, do you have paracetamol)?" I say it unsteadily, copying it from the app on my phone. They understand enough, though my butchered pronunciation had obscured some of the request. I show them what is written on my phone, and they immediately understand. To my relief, the older one speaks a little English, and explains that they do not have it, but gives me directions for another place that did. I decide that I do not have time, as I want to return to Jake as soon as possible. With the help of my phone and gestures, I then ask if they have cold medicine. They do, and I buy a bottle of white pills. The pharmacist from before explains that I need to give him three pills at a time, every couple of hours, preferably with food. This was acceptable, and I give a small bow to demonstrate my gratitude as I pay for the bottle.

The next stop was a konbinni, a Lawson's. I grab some face hygiene masks, and an assortment of soup based meals, as well as a box of sushi. Then I make it back to Jake's. Overall, my whole journey only took about 40 minutes.

I check on him, nothing much has changed. I prepare a glass of water, and rouse him from the bed, bringing a few items with me. He takes three of the white pills, with water, and two pieces of sushi: I determined he did not have an appetite for anything more; otherwise, he would have prepared one of the boxed meals. He lies back down, eyes closed, and I see that his lips are dry. In the bathroom, I find some small hand towels, and using the water I had boiled previously, which was still quite hot, I prepare a lightly damp warm towel, with which I dab against his lips, and gently wipe his forehead, to help break the fever. He sleeps soundly, as I stay by the bedside. I occasionally hum some tunes which I hope sounded soothing, as well as continuing to remoisten his lips a few more times. I gradually hear his breathing relax, and in about three hours he awakens, his face less grim. I proceed to feed him another three pills, and heat up a ramen from the convenience store. He doesn't finish it, but is able to eat about half the bowl, which is a good sign. I put him back to sleep, briefly stroking his back and continuing to hum a few tunes that randomly came to mind. I'm feeling quite tired now, and I drift off into a nap on the carpet by his bedside.

Chapter 11

I hear movement, which jolts me from my nap. Jake is up, and needs to use the bathroom. He walks more steadily than his last bathroom visit earlier. I have collected myself by the time he exits, and I give him another check-up. Complexion is now rosy, though the red-rimmed eyes are a little concerning. His pulse is steadier too, stronger and less shallow/rapid. I ask him how he is feeling, and he sounds more like the Jake I remember. There is still a thickness to his voice, but he sounds better and much less raspy. I'm no doctor but I can say with some confidence that he is on the road to recovery. He agrees and says that he wants to try going to the dojo. It is only around 6 pm, and we can easily make it there in about 20 minutes. The location of Yoseikan Dojo was in Suruga, Mukoshikiji to be precise. I still don't know how to read the maps here, so I can't say if any of those are roads or suburbs, but there was a bus that went past the area, and a short walk would take us there. I express my concerns about him training, mostly as a reconsideration rather than discouragement. But his now bright eyes had their fire restored, as he tells me with the utmost conviction, "I can do this."

The trip is mostly uneventful. He dons the face mask I bought earlier, which helps to preserve his strength and ward off the cold air. We have a slight hiccough as we try to take the bus, our first time in Japan. I didn't realise that everyone has to enter at the back section and either swipe their transit card or take a ticket. I felt bad about holding up these folks probably coming home from a long day, but the bus driver, a petit lady, does her best as I try to communicate the location we are heading to. She also looks blankly as I show her my coins; we find out when we are about to disembark that people paid for their fares at the end, which actually makes more sense to me. I pay the 230 yen required. Poor Jake made another mistake when he throws in a handful of 100 yen pieces all at once, not realising that exact change was the norm. She looks alarmed, and takes out a 1,000-yen note to put into a separate feed, which converts notes to coins. After giving Jake his change, we express our thanks and make it to the dojo, almost walking past it in the dark.

It is next to a café, which closes as we approach. I suppose business was slow tonight, or maybe it just closed early? Sitting in the dark, we wait for the place to open. Soon we are joined by three others, Jake's group from Tokyo who had also come here to train: Gary, Jim and Bryan. Unlike Jake, they are studying or working here, so had come from other commitments. They express some concern about Jake's health, for Jake had not told them he was ill, but are grateful he could make it. Initially greeting me in Japanese, we all laugh when I explain that I am not from here, or even an aikidoka (practitioner of aikido). Jake proudly mentions that I'm his spiritual teacher, which I quickly refute as undue flattery, explaining that while I do a little kung fu, it is for spiritual purposes only. They are all easy going, and are quite excited to be meeting Washizu-sensei, a celebrated master who did international seminars, had written a few books, and also had an instructional video in circulation. We wonder where everyone is, as it is five minutes to 7 pm. As if on cue, a black van then pulls by the dojo and reverses in, where a stout looking man with a shaved head comes out to greet us. A large boy, maybe 19 or 20, steps out of the van too, a little shy at the sight of us. The older man doesn't speak much English, but is unfazed at seeing a bunch of westerners at his dojo. He ushers us inside, out of the cold. Jake explains to me that he wasn't Washizu-sensei, but clearly someone fairly high up on the administrative chain.

After we are inside, I see a well-furbished dojo. We all remove our shoes, and I am told that it is also polite to bow as a sign of respect when stepping onto the main area, where the floors were lined with a type of impact matting. A few brazier style heaters (electric) are placed around the corners closest to the main entrance, slowly heating up as Jake and his guys go to get changed.

The man and boy from earlier start to warm up with falling and rolling drills, and soon there is a lot of people tumbling about. I am sitting on a wicker couch next to the entrance. Before long, other people arrive to join in the training session. One girl (the lone female of the dojo this evening) invites me to join in too, but I explain clumsily that I did not know aikido, and upon hearing my broken Japanese, she switches to clear English. We have a small conversation while she is warming herself (I am sitting next to one of the heaters). I praise her English, but in typical Japanese fashion she modestly shakes her head and claims it is not good, which I try to reassure otherwise.

"*Moto boku no nihongo ga umakatara* (I wish my Japanese was better)," which makes her smile, and I am glad I'm able to communicate it well enough to be understood. She then excuses herself to go change, and I find it funny to see that her training robes, or gi, made her look twice as stocky; I noticed before that she was very slim, an observation which her uniform tried to contradict. As she begins practicing with the others, I notice that she falls very softly, which Jake explains later is due to broken ribs which haven't completely healed yet. These people never cease to amaze me, and I am resolved to adopt some of their work ethics once I return home.

When Washizu arrives, he begins to loosen up by the entrance. He is small, with thinning hair, but there is an unmistakable albeit casual authority in his stride, and his eyes are shrewd and clever. I notice that he walks solidly, yet not heavily, the sign of a well-grounded man, and his breath control is sublime, a sign of inner self-mastery. Jake's group immediately come to greet him, addressing him as Washizu-sama: the suffix 'sama' is an honorific denoting high importance. Jake hands over an envelope which carries the introduction letter Naomi translated, and a lot of cash, which is normal to present as a gift to the school. I count maybe 20 or 30 thousand yen, which I hope is from the entire group, not Jake alone! Washizu-sama reads the letter, and his friendly face expresses mild surprise as he says something to an older man, though all I make out is the phrase 'Jan de Jong'. This older man, whose name is Kozin, speaks English very well, in an older style tinged with a slight British flavour, reminiscent of Received Pronunciation.

The English language contains many variations, not just owing to how it integrated within foreign cultures, but also within the nation itself. Cockney and London accents is common in movies, but Received Pronunciation is the most correct form, considered high class as it was used by typically wealthy and privileged people. The way one spoke was once viewed as a reflection of class, something highlighted in the play *Pygmalion* by George Bernard Shaw, who protested speech-based discriminations for the inaccurate measure they were. Despite this, I enjoyed RP when needing to make a good formal impression, for exactly the same reasons Shaw said we ought not to.

Kozin explains to us that it was surprising to hear Jake's group was comprised of students from the Jan de Jong lineage, Jan de Jong being a Dutch aikido instructor who was well known for trying to experiment with the art during his lifetime.

The class officially begins now that the head instructor has arrived, and I witness the way body mechanics transcended calculations, becoming an expression of pure will. The shaved man who opened the dojo is broad shouldered, and has powerful tripping techniques. Kozin was skilled, but I mostly recall how funny he was by pretending to be injured by various grabs and trips. It helped to put everyone in a relaxed mood. Washizu-sama is amazingly efficient with his movements and could sweep even the biggest, heaviest people there off their feet with relative ease. When one person tried to escape a grounded arm lock, he simply transitioned his smaller body in order to pin them.

After a while of watching them struggle, he would release them, as a fisherman tosses a small fish back into the ocean. I am able to deepen my understanding of physics, specifically energy manipulation, by watching him. The most repeated phrase he used for his students was "Relax!" He was right, I am able to grasp that his strength comes from not forcing it, or imposing his will, but superseding another's. This could be considered the heart of aikido and gave me insights into other philosophies I had studied.

At the end of class, everybody gathers in a circle to engage in several exercises that help their bodies cope with the change in activity levels, and afterwards everyone starts to grab a broom from a pile of brooms in the right-hand corner. They sweep the matting for a while, brushing debris away, and then everyone sits by the very back of the room, near the altar. Kozin helps translate as the new guys introduce themselves. I can feel that they are cementing the bonds which were forged during practice, the steps to becoming part of a community in due time. Photos are taken, and even I am invited to join in, though I did feel it isn't entirely appropriate. The room setting is now more casual as everyone socialises.

Washizu-sama and Kozin are curious about me, an Asian who was friends with a group of westerners who came to their dojo, but did not join in the session. Jake explains that I did kung fu, and begins to demonstrate a palm strike he had learned (with some guidance from me) against a large sand bag hanging nearby. Washizu-sama seems impressed, muttering under his breath something I translate along the lines of 'good power', which I agree with. Kozin asks me which style I practiced, but owing to my lack of formal lineage, I merely give him the name of the style Jake had been learning, hakkyokuken, or bajiquan in Chinese. I am impressed that they know of it, though I suppose martial artists of their experience would have heard of this style. I do not actually practice it in depth, mainly researching it for power generation, but Jake fell in love with the style so I gave him what little I could to experiment with.

After that display, I daresay he was probably better than me now, as I don't practice martial arts nearly as much as he does. However, Washizu-sama goes to his office, and reappears with a beautiful paper fan, one with kanji inscribed. He explains to me that the words were his handwritten calligraphy and philosophy of martial arts: that through our martial paths, friendships could be formed. I am struck with admiration for the simple yet profound message, and thank him as sincerely as I can. It is a powerfully symbolic keepsake, but I decide to give it to Jake as an extra encouragement. The other guys were going to head into Shizuoka for dinner but Jake is still recovering, so declined. Kozin offers us a ride back home, insisting on it when I ask about a taxi (I didn't think it wise to expose Jake to the weather after two hours of training). We are glad to accept, his black SUV is much nicer than a bus and cheaper than a taxi, unless you factored in our gratitude, which was immense. We happily chat about many things on the short ride back. Jake gives him some contact details, and I offer my email, just in case he needed to contact me. As he drops us off we wave goodbye, and he departs with a small honk of his horn.

"A really nice guy, and so funny too!" Jake's experience has left him very cheerful, but I notice a gauntness entering his face now that the excitement was over. We go inside, and I prepare tea and noodles, discarding the leftovers from his late lunch. He takes his pills, and eats heartily, finishing the entire meal to my relief. I am enjoying my potato chips and I drink the coke I got from the Lawson's konbinni earlier. When he is finished, he inspects the fan, and is as thrilled as I envisioned. We don't want to over stimulate him any further, so I suggest it is time to go to bed. I settle on the couch, and am happy to hear snores coming from his room, a peaceful sleep that erased his earlier tortured infirmity. I drift into restfulness, mentally processing what I had seen today. There is something I have to do before going to bed. Taking out my phone, I message Naomi.

Thomas: Hey, I'll be in Osaka pretty soon! Are you still free to hang out on Friday or Saturday?

(I've been really lucky in Japan, she replies within the next 10 minutes instead of 10 hours.)

Naomi: Cool!

I'm working both days, but Saturday is better, more flexible hours. What time do you wanna meet?

Thomas: Lunch? Can you do 1-2pm?

Naomi: Sure.

Thomas: Wait, I meant meet from 1 or 2pm.

I want to spend more than just an hour with you hahah!

Naomi: Yeah, I figured.

'Flips hairs' lol!

1pm then. Where do you wanna meet?

Thomas: Anywhere is fine, really, I'm in Japan to see my dear friend. Nothing in Osaka can top that! Just as long as we can talk and catch up.

Naomi: Let's go to the Yodobashi. 8F, dining level.

Thomas: Awesome, where's that?

Naomi: There's a few around, but one is near Umeda jr. I can meet you there from the 7-11?

Thomas: See you then. Goodnight Naomi!

Naomi: [Sends a gif of a dancing bear]

I don't know what to make of the dancing bear, but I am more focused on the conversation leading up to it. It was happening, a time and place had been set aside, and we would see each other in a few days. I am almost too excited to fall asleep, but I recall Washizu's words, and I do my best to relax. Sleep eventually does come to me, but in that time I had overanalysed the situation. What would seeing her again be like? Would it feel like old times, or would conversation be made awkward by the years apart? Did she suspect why I had come to see her? Could I go through with telling her my true feelings? And most puzzling of all, what did the bear mean???

Chapter 12

I wake up before Jake does, and use the bathroom. Checking my phone in the dim light, I am surprised that it is already past 8 am. Come to think of it, the curtains everywhere I've been to in Japan have been unusually effective in keeping out sunlight. Maybe they realise that darkness is better for deep sleep (which is better for you), or maybe it is the thoroughness of their interior decorators. It is really comfortable, and I almost feel like it turned the home into one's own private pocket dimension. Unless your neighbours are really loud, and I feel another twinge of regret for what happened at Vik and Maggy's place, not only for the rug but the noise we made. Hopefully, the surrounding houses would let it go, as it was just the one evening. Then again, depending on their sex life, maybe noise wasn't as uncommon as I assumed. I chuckle at the thought, a moment of immature indulgence.

Jake can be heard getting out of bed. He staggers out of the room, stretching and yawning at the same time. A quick look at his complexion tells me he had slept well; there is colour back in his cheeks and a much more vigorous stride in his walk. I greet him,

"*Ohayo* (Mornin')!"

"*Ohayo gozaimasu*, (good morning), Thomas!"

"You look good, let me check your vitals after you freshen up!" He is a stickler for hygiene, and goes through his morning cleansing ritual. When he does come out, I ask him to sit on the couch and steady his breathing. There is still a slight disturbance in his lungs, nothing like pneumonia but still a slight concern. His temperature is down, the throat no longer feels dry or sore, and his heart rate seems good, though I detect that there is a residual weakness under the stronger rhythm. He would be fine though, with more rest. I ask him if he is hungry, as recovering drains the body of a lot of energy, and as a slim man he didn't have ample reserve to rely on.

"Yes, I know a great udon place around here actually, I insist on taking you there!" His jovial nature has returned, and I am all too pleased to see he has an appetite. I wait for him to change clothes, as I am already in my standard attire, and we head out.

This morning wasn't sunny, though the pale light here was probably also a reflection of Shizuoka's fishing industry: we are relatively close to the harbour from Jake's. A quaint little shop is where Jake escorts me, and inside we are greeted before taking a seat by the street window. I am intrigued by a picture in the menu, and order a tofu udon while Jake orders a beef udon. We refresh ourselves with chilled water and make simple conversation until the food arrives. Two giant bowls, each the size of a medium wok, are brought to us, and my suspicions are confirmed: the tofu was a thin slice, fried, and slightly larger than the size of my hand, which is quite impressive as I have large ones; Vik has compared my hands to garden trowels. Jake's meal was a standard udon, though the beef looked almost delicate in the huge bowl, as they were lightly pan seared and cut into thin strips. It smelled delicious, beckoning to us as we separate the bamboo chopsticks they gave us, preparing to dig in.

"*Itadakimasu!*" we said in unison. This phrase is uttered at the beginning of a meal, much like saying grace before a meal, but I had not seen it very much since arriving in Tokyo. Yet as Jake and I are celebrating the success of last night, we indulge ourselves with a slight bit of cultural assimilation. I taste a spoonful of soup, it is sweeter than a ramen broth, most of the udon I've tried is, but there is something in the aroma which hinted at a savouriness I had yet to identify. I tear off a piece of my tofu's corner, and find it sweet, the taste possibly augmented by the soup. The noodles are good, texture not too soft, and we spend the next few minutes occupied with slurping and chewing.

"Thank you, Thomas, I think I would have died if it hadn't been for you yesterday."

"Please, you were barely incapacitated, though I am glad you recovered enough to go. They all seemed very impressed, and I hope you get to train at max power soon."

"Yeah, but last night I don't think they were impressed by me, compared to the other guys. I was probably too nervous too, Washizu kept telling me to relax but I was tensing on instinct!"

"Oh yeah, he was saying that to everyone though hahah! I think you did well, and you have the videos I took with your phone to prove it. In fact, I heard them mention that you had good power! I suppose you watched them last night instead of going to bed straightway, like I suggested?" I raise my brows in mock sternness, but smile, which robs the expression of any weight.

"A little, heh. But I will review them properly later. Speaking of which, what are you doing today?"

"Well, my plan was to go and visit the grave of Tokugawa Ieyasu, it's located at a shrine which is not too far by bus. But I also really want to head into Kyoto, as I have to check into my Osaka hotel tonight, and Kyoto is on the way to Osaka."

"Can I come to Kyoto with you?" The question takes me by surprise, but then again, Jake didn't have to study or work here, like the other training buddies, so it made sense that he had more free time. Still, I had my reservations.

"In Kyoto, I plan to travel up to the top of Fushimi Inari Taisha, the famous vermillion gates shrine of the God Inari. It's 223 meters above sea level. You just recovered, so I don't know if your lungs can handle it. But we can go visit Tokugagwa's shrine together?"

"Nah, I don't want to miss out on a trip to Kyoto. Come on, let's go up and conquer the mountain!" He coughs while declaring this, which only stresses my earlier point. But if he feels like it, why not? The elderly make it up Mt Inari frequently, and even now, I'm certain he is healthier than a senior citizen. Hang on, what if Japanese senior citizens were fitter than their western counterparts? He looks at me to give him my blessing.

"Hmmm… okay, but you keep taking that medicine. It's probably a very powerful placebo, especially as I got it for you. Speaking of which, I wish we remembered to bring it with us for you to take now."

"No problems, I brought it with me!" He pulls out the bottle and gulps it down with water. Jake is young but thorough, I couldn't fault him that, so I relinquish any remaining hesitations and we return to his apartment to get my belongings. One would not normally bring their luggage to a mountaintop, but I will not be returning to Shizuoka, and my luggage is extremely light for a winter vacation. It will be no trouble to carry everything to the mountaintop with me.

We then take a bus to the JR station, before catching a bullet to Kyoto. It doesn't take more than two hours, and from there, it is only a short connection to get to the Inari shrine, on the Nara line. The train is packed, and I am apologetic when we are forced to wedge ourselves against a group of young girls. I am pleased for Jake though, I like to think he is enjoying being squished up against young ladies, but he looks uncomfortable, almost as if he doesn't want to be mistaken for a pervert. Another good thing about the ride is being in the front compartment, as I get to see the conductor work. Our train is something out of children's picture book, an older model, and lime green too! Even the pace felt scenic, as it was going at a decent speed without the distinct zooming sensations of a modern train.

Once we get there, I am able to appreciate the magnitude of Kyoto's, and possibly Japan's, most iconic shrine. There are tourists as far as the eye can see, and outside the station, across the road, lie the entrance to the shrine grounds. Fushimi Inari Taisha was dedicated to Inari, who was the god of the harvest, prosperity and by association, fertility. It has over 10,000 torii gates, which kind of look like the mathematical symbol Pi (Pythagoras). Apparently, that number is growing because businesses pay for more to be added, as they are a symbol of good luck. The vermillion colour is said to ward off bad luck, and I immediately feel a strong, if somewhat commercialised, spiritual connection to this place. Maybe it is the gates themselves, which are said to bridge the natural and supernatural worlds, or the fact that everything here is so very Japanese, but I am immediately drawn to the place and couldn't wait to explore.

Jake and I wander through the crowds, and I am fascinated at the number of people dressed in traditional robes, a colourful pink and blue with flowers (for the ladies), and dark blue or brown robes for the guys. They are even sporting the traditional sandals with white socks! I take a picture of one particularly beautiful couple who indulge me, before I realise that these people don't work here, they are probably just tourists who hired the costumes as a bonus element for the visit.

One of the most memorable features for me is the honouring rite, and the purification rituals. Since my childhood, I have always held a deep reverence for the rituals involved in spiritual and religious ceremonies. Here, I could practice the Shinto rituals I had researched; Google counts as research, right? The correct ways to pay respect at the shrines was to lowly bow twice, clap your hands twice, and spend a moment in reflection, or making a wish, before bowing once more. Then you can shake the bells which hang off ropes, and make a donation too if you so wished. I suppose the gods here understand the nature of greasing the wheels, or maybe a donation represented sincerity and commitment to one's desires. Then again, history might comment that religion and profiteering aren't as removed from each other as they claim to be. Regardless, as a novelty, I have all my coins in my pocket, to be doled out as we make our way up the mountain.

The base, as previously mentioned, is where the majority of the souvenir shops are located. There was even a section where fortunes could be read using a system of numerology, but they did not offer English translations so we didn't bother. I'm sorely tempted to buy myself a fox mask, but can't find one that would fit me properly. Unlike the samurai helmet and mask, it appears I did not get lucky here. There are statues of foxes, or kitsune in Japanese, EVERYWHERE. Foxes are sacred to Inari, who employs them as messengers and servants. I wonder if I can see any here, as we make our way through to the pathways that lead up to the peak. A Shinto priest, in a brilliant white robe and black hat, is conducting a ceremony with other acolytes, and we observe for a moment before passing on.

Jake is annoyed that the crowds prevent him from taking some ideal photos, but they noticeably thin as we get progressively higher. Still plenty of traffic, though now they are spaced out more pleasantly, and add to the scenery rather than drew attention from it. Along our way up, we encounter a man and someone who could have been his girlfriend: I found it funny to watch them, as he is clearly tired and can't be bothered making a decent pace, while in contrast she is energetic and went on ahead of him, often calling on him to pick up the pace. He sighs, and imperceptibly increases his rate, these steps clearly too much for him.

I see different resting points along the track, which give a space for less fit travellers to sit and breathe. There are also some tea houses/restaurants open on the path, and perhaps unsurprisingly there are plenty of vending machines around here too. I'm glad that if we are in want of a drink, they are readily available here. Shops sell iconic wares, such as green tea products, candles, as well as charms and fortunes. One can even buy a miniature torii gate as a memento of their trip.

I have to say that the air is amazingly clear and pure. The resting spaces have shrines too; in fact numerous small shrines are available along the track, and many have a purification fountain. This is something I cannot resist, and I frequently stop to conduct the ritual. Jake is curious, and asks me what it is for, so I get him to do it too. We take a ladle with our right hands, and fill it with water from the basin, pouring it over left hands, before switching hands and repeating the process. Then we take the ladle in our right hands again, and tip some water into our left hands, to carry the water to our mouths. It is improper to touch the ladle with our mouths, and probably unhygienic considering the millions of people who visit here each year. Rinsing our mouths with the chilled, refreshing waters, we spit into a lower tray/basin, before returning the ladles to their resting spot. I feel better with each purification, as if I'm unburdening my spirit as well as washing it out. Jake is much more interested in the surroundings than spiritual cleansing, so he doesn't engage much more after his first try.

About half way up the mountain, we see a fork, and take the right hand side. Not too far ahead, the path opens into a clearing, another resting spot, but this one overlooks the city of Kyoto. Jake is doing fine, he has his filter mask back on but other than that is looking as vigorous as anyone did going up a mountain. Neither of us needs to stop, but we do, just to drink in the spectacular view from this vantage point. I also engage in another purification ritual, though Jake declines as the waters are a little cold for him. We continue our way up, occasionally stopping to read information and history signs that can be found at some of the shrines. At last, we make it to the top of the mountain.

The original shrine to Inari is simple and mostly a collection of stone monuments surrounding an altar. It is not architecturally impressing, compared to the newer temple shrines at the base, but it literally represented hundreds of years of history, which give it a certain gravitas. There is even a record of past emperors who had visited this place and given it their blessing, while being blessed by the priests in turn. Jake explores the area, and finds a cat that he attempts to follow, to take a picture of. I have almost run out of coins on the journey here, but I saved my last one, a 500-yen piece, to offer as I approach the altar, and I kneel to pray. Initiating a few breathing exercises, I gather my thoughts, and try to commune with the local deity.

I am not a follower of Shinto, though perhaps you will look favourably upon me due to the years I spent promoting Zen. I am in Japan, and this place has revitalised me. I do not feel so washed out and faded, I am emboldened, but also slightly afraid of seeing my friend. She and I will reunite after years apart. Though we have corresponded in that time, I am here because I feel a great, tremulous, need to see her, to make sense of how I feel. I don't have many people to talk to about my thoughts, being a private man who hides under bravado. Many people come to me for counsel, yet my best friend is no longer in my life and I felt a little lost without him.

Actually, it was similar to how I felt when she, the one I'm seeing soon, left all those years ago.

Am I too dependent on others for self-worth? This is probably not in your forte, but the truth is, I just wanted to make it out as if I was undertaking a pilgrimage, and your shrine ended up being the one where I reflect upon my troubles. Hopefully, you can act as a catalyst for the actualisation and validation of my inner feelings. Oh wait, am I supposed to make a wish or something now? I just paid my respects at the lesser shrines below, but I guess up here I should ask for something...

I consider many things, including asking Inari to help Naomi accept my feelings if she could. Or maybe I could just ask for world peace? It might be likelier, hah. Eventually, I do make my request, one that has more to do with my own convictions than belief in Inari's power.

I wish that Naomi is happy and in good health for as long as she can be, that she prospers in her career, and one day finds a man befitting her to start a wonderful family with, if that's what she wants? Oh, and also, maybe I should ask for Jake to get a girlfriend? A cool and pretty girl he could enjoy hanging out with regularly. Also, last thing I promise, when I return home, please, let me find my Zen after all this is over?

Arigatou gozaimasu (thank you very much).

I asked for three things, but I don't want to treat the shrine like a genie or anything like that, it's just nice to vent my thoughts. I bow low and maintain my position for a time. When I open my eyes, I see that Jake has returned and is watching me. I smile, and ask him if he is done chasing cats, to which he nods. I take in the view one last time, and indicate we should return to the mountain base.

"Then let's go back down!"

He didn't find that cat, and we didn't see any real foxes either. But there is more wildlife as we go down the other side of the mountain, such as koi fish in ponds, birds feeding on grains, and even a sign warning any night-time visitors that boars had been seen in the area! Also, to everyone's delight (we were now seeing the pedestrian traffic thicken once more), we encounter more cats around this part of the mountain. There are speckled cats, white and brown cats, even a proud black cat that looks at us thoughtfully before disappearing into the forest area. Jake also sees a bundle of kittens which are huddled together in the most adorable fashion, possibly to keep warm. He tries to alert this to a group of pretty girls dressed in kimonos, but they only politely stare. Once we are walking away, we hear a delighted squeal as the girls found the kitten cluster, and we hear a joyous utterance of "*Neko-chan* (Kitty cat)!" Jake is disappointed, as I suppose he wanted to curry favour with the girls, so I try to lighten his mood by teaching him a phrase from my book: 'gai koku jin dakara'.

"What's that mean?"

"It means 'Is it because I'm a foreigner?' It might come in handy!"

He memorises this phrase which seems to resonate within him. He repeats it slowly, to get a feel for it.

"*Gai ko-ku jin da-kara?*"

"Nah, I just think the girls weren't used to hearing you speak Japanese, maybe next time you should just say 'neko' and point."

"Next time I'll respond with 'gai koku jin dakara'." We laugh, he is no longer hung up about what happened, and we make our way down.

Near the base of this mountainside, we see more Buddhist shrines, as opposed to Shinto ones. There is a golden statue of Kannon, or Guan Yin, the goddess of mercy. I am familiar with her, thanks to my grandfather's Buddhist heritage and my childhood years spent playing in the shed. I stop to pay my respects, in a Buddhist fashion rather than a Shinto one. An attractive woman in her mid-20s asks me, in clear English, if I could help her take a photo. She is using a traditional film roll camera instead of her phone, and I do my best to get a clear shot. She thanks me, we maintain eye contact for a bit longer than necessary, and I sense that we could have talked more, maybe over a drink, but I'm too subdued from the journey to flirt, so I only smile, and wish her a good day. Eventually, we make it to the start of our journey, the marketplace. Jake considers a few wares, but as I cannot find an appropriate mask, I do not buy anything, the experience being sufficient. We head back to Kyoto central.

Chapter 13

The day is giving way to night, and we had skipped lunch. But Jake is a connoisseur; that is to say he had a more discerning palate. When I suggest we just eat at the train station he dismisses the idea, and we begin a hunger induced walk around the area. His instincts were right on the money, as the moment we step out of Kyoto station, we find a massive Buddhist temple, with huge gates and a lotus fountain display at the front. He teases me, rightfully,

"And you wanted to stay in the train station!"

I am too taken back by the scope of this temple to respond, so I could only concur by nodding.

We continue to explore Kyoto, and after an hour of walking, Jake settles our sights on an upscale looking restaurant. I am quite hungry now, so I agree to it. Even though I would have eaten anywhere, I have to admit that this place has a very appetising aroma. It boasts a luxurious yet modest décor that I find very pleasing to admire while looking at the menu. Jake and I are seated next to two Korean girls, who eye us with some interest. I glance briefly, grin and greet them with "Anasayo (Hello)" which makes them giggle, before they turn back to their meal. Coincidently, both of our tables require an English menu, and seeing that put me at ease as this place is foreigner friendly.

We soon learn from the manager, who comes to serve us personally, that this place was well known for their sukiyaki, which is a form of clay pot cuisine. Unlike steamboat clay pot, where the raw food is cooked in a broth, sukiyaki involved cooking the raw food in a fermented sauce. I am also delighted to see that we were cooking on live coals, and not an electric grill. It made the whole experience more authentic.

I also order a rice dish, as well as fries, which arrive on a little platter with aioli sauce. It is crunchy, and the aioli is light without being bland. Jake declines more than one fry, as he is a man of taste. The rice dish comes with a little clay teapot, and I discover that this is for us to pour in with our rice. It is called ochazuke, meaning to 'submerge in tea'. The manager explains that though it is ochazuke, here the tea is replaced with dashi broth, a very light soup that made for a more savoury substitute. Very interesting concept, I have heard of a tea that uses roasted rice grains, but this is my first encounter with rice that is eaten in a tea broth. Or whatever dashi is. It is light, yet still filling to a degree, and fragrant too.

Our sukiyaki platter arrives: pork rashers, onions, mushrooms, tofu, and a heap of green shallots. I take over the cooking process, so that Jake can focus on eating. He finds it surprising that we cook our own food, but enjoys the experience all the same. I do not eat pork, but I dip the tofu and vegetable into the egg and yam sauce respectively, which I find adds some diversity to the flavours. To both of our surprise, we enjoy eating the shallots, which are tender and sweet after being cooked in the sauce. Clearly I've been doing it wrong all this time.

Seeing that we are nearly done, the two Korean girls lean forwards to get our attention. They have it without much effort, and soon we are striking up a conversation. One of them has curly, medium length jet-black hair, and wears glasses; her English is better than her friend's, who has long straight hair, dyed reddish brown, which frame her delicate features. After Jake and I say hello, we discuss the meal.

They are surprised to hear that it is our first time eating sukiyaki, and commended us on a pretty decent job. I jokingly explain that the only reason for that was because we were watching them, and copying what they did. They find this funny, though Kimi, the one with glasses, has to explain it for her friend Soo Jung. I ask them if they are on holiday, they explain that they were students at Kyoto University, and lived around there. They didn't speak Japanese especially well yet, so had been using the English Kimi knew in order to get by. We smile understandably, being in the same position. When they ask if we are on holiday I say I am, but my friend is staying in Skizuoka for a month to train in aikido. It turns out that Soo Jung did hapkido, which is a Korean martial art that also focused on joint locks, though apparently included more strikes.

I think I sense Jake falling for this girl the moment he heard she did a martial art, which is great as she is very pretty, but I didn't want looks to be the only factor. He has told me otherwise on separate occasions but I'm certain he would change his mind after exploring the dating scene. I decide to do my best to play wingman, and in that moment I could almost feel a sense of camaraderie in Kimi, who seemed more laid back than Soo Jung, and seemed to read my cues well.

Jake and I decide to get crepes afterwards, and I ask if the girls would like to join us, which they accept. We ask for the cheque, thank the manager for the meal at his lovely establishment, and make our way to a dessert joint Jake had seen on our search before. It is quiet, with only a single girl in a black café uniform at the counter, and she is in the middle of cleaning machines. Upon our arrival, she switches between that task and greets us, doing it so seamlessly that I seriously thought she was expecting people, and had just gotten bored in the waiting process. Jake insists on covering everyone, and I allow him to cover me so as to make the girls more comfortable in accepting too.

We get a strawberry crepe for him, a Nutella and banana crepe for me, and the girls each get a chocolate crepe. I'm surprised to find that the crepes come wrapped up much like an ice cream cone, but it is apparently normal to Kimi and Soo Jung, so I observe their technique. I almost eat the paper it is wrapped in, and do tear a pierce off with my teeth, but we all find it funny as I play around with my food. I am hoping my antics serve to make Jake look better, and I do think that Soo Jung is likely interested in him. Once the two of them get over their shyness (or language barrier?) I think they might be able to connect better. Thinking about what we saw on the walk before dinner, I recall the ideal location to unwind.

"Hey, let's go to the arcade!"

This arcade is located around the corner, upstairs. As in, the stairs just lead from the entrance outside to the second floor. After a quick scout around, Jake sees a fighting game console, at the same time Soo Jung does. Inserting 100 yen (50 per person), she takes a seat with him as they begin to play. I watch for a bit, before leaving to get some change, and returning with 1,000-yen worth of coins for them to continue playing. She is good, and nearly wins the first game. She is also competitive, and insists on a rematch. Kimi and I leave them to it, and we wander through the place with a casual interest. Kimi breaks the comfortable silence first.

"You are a good friend." I smile, and she continues.

"My friend thought Jake was cute, but when you spoke Korean to us, we were worried you overheard us." I remember the giggle from earlier, so that was why.

"Hah don't worry, I only know how to say hello! I'm glad you speak English so well, otherwise we wouldn't have been able to enjoy ourselves tonight." She smiles but insists her English isn't good. Maybe I'm too westernised, the Asian standard of 'good' isn't what I was used to. Kimi continues,

"How old are you guys?"

"I'm turning 29 in a few days. Jake is turning 22 this year, I think. And how about you ladies? You said university before, so I assume 20 to 22?"

"Close! Soo Jung and I are 23 this year, but I am still 22. Wow, almost 30? I can believe, but you still look like you're in your mid-20s."

"You're too kind! I'm still 28, though I'm not a young man for much longer! Does Soo Jung like younger men? Jake is very mature for his age." She purses her lips, and tilts her glasses to think, then smiles.

"We find out soon!" We laugh at this, and she is about to say something, but Jake and Soo Jung approach us. Soo Jung raises her brows and says something to Kimi in Korean, to which Kimi blushes and says something else in a flustered manner, waving her hands. Was it about me? Instead of wondering, I look at Jake and ask him,

"Who won?" The girls stop their conversation and Soo Jung smiles, at which Jake smiles too.

"It was a draw." I nod, impressed, as Jake knew his way around many fighting console games. He's often invited me to join him, but I really don't have much interest in video games. It was getting late, so we walk the girls to the subway. They are speaking more in Korean now, so Jake and I have our own conversation. I clarify the outcome of the game.

"Wow, she's that good to draw with you, huh?" He leans in and whispers,

"She's definitely good, but I let her win in the last one so it would be a draw. I'm a gentleman, like you've always encouraged me to be." I raise my brows and smirk. So sneaky, my young apprentice! The conversation then turns to how he is getting home: a simple Kyoto Shinkansen to Shizuoka. Easy and direct. I, on the other hand, would need to take the Shinkansen to Shin-Osaka, then take a train to Osaka from there, before taking a subway to Tanimachiyonchome, and walking to my hotel. Still, from Kyoto that wasn't so bad, and I was arguably going to take the same amount of time as Jake to get home. We make it to subway, and the girls give each of us a hug. Soo Jung lingers a bit with Jake, and even gives him a peck him on the cheek. Kimi and I have less romantic farewell, but she before letting go, whispers in my ear,

"Don't tell your friend, but Soo Jung let him win before." I start laughing in fits; they are made for each other. I decide against telling Kimi that Jake had done the same, but I couldn't help occasionally chuckling as we made it to the JR station. Jake is in a daze, and doesn't respond much to me, I assume that being kissed by a pretty girl does that to anyone. I ensure he makes it to the right platform before we part, and he seems almost himself again.

"Thank you, Thomas! This was such an awesome day!" I smile as he boards the train, before saying to no one in particular,

"And to think, I wanted to stay inside the train station…"

I begin to make it to the platform for Shin-Osaka, then Osaka, then to the subway system for Tanimachiyonchome, which was written as Tanimachi-4-chome (I realised on the ride here that 'yon' denotes '4' in Japanese). From there I wander around, noting that there is a McDonald's nearby, and even a Family Mart on the street corner opposite the hotel. I go in there, to buy myself a packet of potato chips, and some coke, before queuing at reception. I was lucky tonight, apparently the reception at this place, MyStays Osaka, closes at 10 pm, which was about 10 minutes away. I check in, grab my keycard, and make my way to the room.

My first impression is wow, I had a kitchen! My second impression? This place is bigger than the standard room in a Japanese hotel, even bigger than the room I had at the Fuji Premium Resort. I enter, fiddle with the hot water (which has to be manually activated) and take a shower, ecstatic that this place gave me a **free bathrobe**! The hot water is a bit temperamental, but eventually I get that sweet spot between freezing and scalding. While waiting for my hair to dry, I check my luggage; it is very light now, for all I carry are a spare set of clothes, knick knacks I had picked up, and Naomi's present, which is undamaged despite being dragged throughout Japan and three airports. I carefully store them in the closet compartments, where they would be temporarily housed for the last time. Soon they would change hands, and my luggage would be as unburdened as my heart. Maybe. Hopefully.

Chapter 14

Getting up at around 11 am, I decide that it's time for me to just chill and unwind. Though the winter conditions did not freeze me, I had taken some exposure damage from the sun, as well as the dehydrating nature of the cold. I didn't want to see Naomi tomorrow looking blistered, so I go to the Family Mart to see if I could find any moisturizer. Moments later, I walk out with a 30ml tube of goat's milk skin conditioner. Returning to my hotel, I apply the lotion on my face and prepare a moist face towel to cover me while I meditate in bed.

I'm seeing Naomi tomorrow. I had today left to try and gather my thoughts, as well as do some sightseeing while I could. My flight is tomorrow evening and leaves at midnight; does that count as tomorrow or the day after? I need to be at the airport by the late evening tomorrow, so I guess I should say I'm flying out tomorrow instead of the day after... sigh, I'm rambling. I take a deep breath through the cloth, its moisture makes the air I take in heavy, but that ballast is a good thing for I am forced to breathe out completely in order to clear my lungs.

It is simple in theory: *Naomi, I have to tell you that I love you, and I haven't stopped loving you since before you left.* No, that's too blunt. *Naomi, I hope this doesn't change anything, but I love you.* That is worse, how the hell is 'I love you' not meant to change anything between people? Besides, am I really hoping that nothing would change between us? If I'm being honest, a part of me will be happy if she feels the same way, but that would lead to a whole new vein of uncertainties. Better do what I do best –

procrastinate. What was there to do here anyway? I get up and get dressed before getting outside.

The great thing about my hotel? It is within walking distance of one of Osaka's most renowned tourist attractions: Osaka Castle! The old capital, a historical setting that had lasted to the modern era. I'm quite excited to explore the grounds and make my way there.

Earlier when I put on the clothes that had been with me for almost all of my stay in Japan, I am a little sad to find that I had lost a button on my coat, somewhere between here and Tokyo. But at least I have my scarf to hide the damage should I need to, though that made me too warm, even when I'm outdoors.

There are plenty of people as I make my way through Osaka, particularly around my hotel. I almost feel as if I am in the central business district back home. I pass by a hospital, which Google Maps tell me is one used to train nursing students. I cross the road, heading to the nature reserve which is where the castle is situated. There are three major parts to the tourist attractions: the castle, the shrine, and the commercial building, called the Kinzo Storehouse.

The castle itself is located within its own grounds, which are surrounded by a moat. Just opposite the bridge that leads inside the building is a Shinto shrine, where some food stalls are located. An old man sits by the gate, playing a shamisen, a type of Japanese lute, at the entrance to the shrine. I cannot help but spend a few minutes listening to the ghostly folk tunes which are both uplifting and haunting, an audio anachronism for the tourists who enjoy the music without realising how it takes them back to the original Osaka Castle. I drop a few coins for his performance, but I do not head into the shrine area yet, I want to explore the castle first.

The fee is only 600 yen for adults, and I gladly pay for a ticket from the machines at the entrance; the ticket is picturesque, with a photo of the castle overlooking the moat. As I approach it, it becomes even more magnificent, a testament to the times when structural integrity and aesthetics were equal partners. The building style is distinctly oriental, and the white walls serve to supplement the gold features and edgings. If I apply a liberal dose of artistic license, I would say that it is almost like a collection of masts that overlap in such a way as to inspire a very well ordered wave motif. The stones used are truly hewn from the rocky earth, not like the brickwork of modern buildings, which seem tame and impotent compared to this stunning majesty of Osaka Castle. Forgive the fanboying, this place is rather awe-inspiring.

I patiently queue, but I soon realise that there are two lines, one for those who wish to use the elevator, and those who are fine with taking the stairs. The elevator only goes to the very top floor, so a lot of people, namely senior citizens, are waiting to go up, and explore the castle as they make their way down. I saw crowds of people, mostly Chinese and Korean, with the exception of schoolchildren, who I hear conversing in Japanese. An assorted speck of westerners could occasionally be seen, few and far between: I detected French and Italian, but I'm certain there are more than that there, as I distinctly hear some forms of Scandinavian as I make my way through.

The main floors are filled with a multitude of paintings, statues, and historical recollections. Floors 3 and 4 prohibit photography or filming, but the policy is largely ignored as the tourists frequently take digital souvenirs. Out of ignorance, not disrespect, I'm sure. On one of the higher levels, I become interested in a teahouse being displayed, noted to be a favourite pastime of Hideoyoshi, the first administrator after Nobunaga's death. Water fountains can be found in the corners of every other floor, and there are three-dimensional screenings of historical events. The attention to detail is impressive, and I wonder if the fight scenes incorporated people like the samurai I saw in Tokyo. But for the most part the re-enactments are of dramatic stage nature, portraying very little action sequences, even when they did depict armies riding out to war.

On the highest level, I find the souvenir shop, with fans and keychains and wrapped gifts much like I saw in the

Samurai Museum. I go outside, sliding open the massive screen door, to take in Osaka from this magnificent viewpoint. Despite the scenery, what I remember most about being up there was a schoolboy yelling out to his teacher, who was outside, on the ground level.

"SENSEIIII!!!!" he would call out to his teacher repeatedly.

To add to my shock, his teacher responds, all the way from the ground floor, which placates the boy. I find it hilarious, his youthful spirit is infectious. It is time to make my way down, and out, which is quicker than going up. Gravity does play its part in this but I would also attribute the extra speed to a combination of that boy's antics, and the fact that I had now seen what was on each floor. I go outside, and notice a wishing well, so drop a coin in, but it is a few seconds before I hear it making impact with the bottom, a soft *thunk* that resonated from the depths of that dark chasm. I depart, and cross the bridge to explore the other side of the grounds, which I had briefly glimpsed earlier.

My time in the shrine is spent peacefully, though after Kyoto, the main appeal of this place is the melody of that old musician, who plays ever a tale of the times long past, and seems to perform for himself as much as the crowds. I give him as much as I can afford. A few birds, pigeons and finches, are gathered near the stalls, feeding on the scraps indulgent tourists threw. Done here, I go to the next destination, the most modern of the three tourist attractions: the Kinzo building.

Inside the first floor is an entire row of different shops, selling merchandise as well as food. There is even a store that sells powdered green tea items, such as cakes, soaps and candles. And green tea of course. I enjoy browsing through the stores, and am tempted by the weaponry at the Ninja Shop. If Jake was here, he would enjoy it on many more levels that I could, but I still think I did a good job of appreciating the wares. How do I know retail was taken seriously in Japan? The staff are dressed in ninja outfits, including the female staff, who are wearing kunoichi outfits.

Very tasteful ones, a little revealing, and for some reason the men shopping here all found it very appealing. Jake might argue that it wasn't authentic, but even he could appreciate the 'dedication' on display here. I wanted to send him a picture, but the thought of him happily playing video games with Soo Jung made me reconsider. It would be a waste of my matchmaking efforts.

Then there is another store, located at the most left hand side of the main entrance (the ninja store was located to the right just as you walk in). This one sold beautifully crafted coin purses, fans, jewellery, and a variety of plushies. Not unreasonably priced, though the coin purses were cheaper at the Tokyo Samurai Museum. I want to get a set of handkerchiefs, but reconsider as I had decided to abstain from souvenirs; my yukata was enough. Besides, I need to get lunch, not make purchases on an empty stomach, it was already close to 4 pm too.

Deciding to stop by the restaurant at the end of the right-hand path, I order some octopus balls, or takoyaki. It is a dish I enjoyed with friends back home, and I recalled Jake's first time.

*A takoyaki ball is served freshly cooked, with sauced octopus meat inside said ball, and topped with dried flakes, mayonnaise and a drizzle of soy sauce. Now, freshly made equates to **steaming** on the inside. It was Jake's first time too, as Oscar had tried it before, so he decided to copy Oscar's example. My stoic friend has a knack for hot foods, be it literal or spicy, and simply puts an entire ball into his mouth, chewing and swallowing. I found it odd, but as Oscar didn't react, I assumed that it was because the serving was not as fresh, and had cooled down. I was wrong, as Jake proved by taking one, biting into it, and almost convulsing due to the steam that was practically bursting forth from the ball! I quickly grab a serviette from him to spit it out, and he spends the next 15 minutes cooling his mouth with water before he reattempts to eat takoyaki, albeit more cautiously. When I queried Oscar afterwards the man just shrugs,* *insisting that it wasn't that hot. I guess years of being hit in the head dulls all the sensations. But it was an experience that practically gave Jake PTSD whenever we ate it again.*

I get in addition to my takoyaki platter some fries and a cup of green tea. At this place, customers can personally adjust the toppings, which they offer in great variety, so I have fun with the soy, mayonnaise, seaweed, and a generous helping of the wafer thin flakes iconic to the dish. My fries are good, crunchier than normal, and I particularly enjoy the thick ketchup that accompanied them. The tea is welcome, as the meal made me thirsty. It is remarkable, but the food here must contain no unnecessary fats, for I had not felt bloated since I arrived. When I return home, I had to start using less salt and oil in my cooking, or maybe I could just move permanently to Japan.

Several moments pass by before I finish indulging my imagination, thinking of what I would do here with Vik and Maggy, and I suppose I could hang out more often with Naomi, though I would probably try to stay close to my xiong di in Zushi, and she did live several hours away, here in Osaka. But what could I do here? I wasn't qualified for anything, though I could try to teach English. If there is something I prided myself on, it was my literary ability, but being a proper teacher is not something I had ever considered doing as a profession. Deep down, I know, and always believe, that the role is not something I'm worthy of until at least another decade of life experiences. While I continue to muse over a life I know would never exist outside of pleasant fancies, I know now that it is time for me to go to my next destination – Dotobori.

Chapter 15

Seeing as it is a Friday night, I will be seeing her tomorrow! I just want to put my mind at ease somehow and not come across as a jittery bundle of nerves, especially as this is our first meeting in years. The guy who met her long ago was prone to nervous enthusiasm, but the man who he had become in six years surely could not allow himself to present a similarly paltry first impression. So with that in mind, I head off to the clubbing district of Osaka.

Calling it the clubbing district is probably incorrect, I'm in the Namba area, I think. While a lot of clubs I Googled are situated around there, the most famous tourist attraction is definitely the Dotonbori Canal. I discover that Dotonburi is famous for the cuisine culture too; the Japanese term for this love of food is kuidaore, or 'buy so much food that you fall into financial ruin'! I chuckle to myself, memorising that word for later use. The sun is setting, and twilight encroaches. I take the subway line closest to my hotel in Tanimachiyonchome, and arrive about 20 minutes later. Osaka is colourful, something that I had discovered by walking around my hotel neighbourhood, but even so, I was taken back at the illumination that greeted me in Dotonbori!

Street vendors and other establishments seem to be arranged by a stage director, with a size and visual coordination that are drawing me in, despite the crowded pedestrian traffic. I see massive signs and billboards that took up an entire side of skyscrapers, and so many people walking around everywhere. I stand on the bridge, named Ebisubashi, to take in my surroundings, feeding on the ambience. Dotonburi has its origins in an ambitious merchant during the early 1600s, who pooled all his wealth in order to undertake the project. Unfortunately, Doton, the businessman with a dream, never lived to see it completed, owing to his death in the Battle of Osaka, but his relations completed the project and named it Dotonbori, or Doton's Canal, in his honour. Apparently, it used to be an entertainment district, which included numerous playhouses and theatres, but after World War 2, that aspect fell into decline. Bombings tend to have that effect I suppose. So it was now more famous for the kuidaore culture that I previously mentioned.

I spent maybe 20 minutes there lost in my thoughts, the cool air and neon glow of the surroundings provide a scenic environment for me to roost. I wonder if Naomi ever came here. She loved to try different foods, and her spirit of adventure had always made her very proactive. I see a few couples walking along the bridge, some are holding boxes of various local cuisines, though they do not sample the food as they walk: it is apparently bad manners here to eat while travelling. I will have to ask her why when I see her, if I remembered or still cared about it. Will she walk with me, on this bridge? Not just for sightseeing, but to share an experience? Or maybe it is something she wouldn't feel comfortable with; I think about all the times she had declined to spend time alone together, back when we did live in the same country.

Maybe she has someone else in her life now, who she did all those couple things with. I'm not sure how I will react to seeing him (if he existed), but I had long accepted that she was far too attractive to stay single, even if people were pining away after her. Not me personally, hah, but I'm fairly certain there were others who felt the same way I did, though perhaps not as strongly. I'd like to think no one else could feel what I feel for her...

Mostly, I worried about whether or not such a man would treat her the way she deserved. I imagine that he was tall, handsome and motivated, someone who could make her laugh as well as challenge her to grow as a person. Could I have been such a man, if I tried? No matter how subjective the criteria, I could never measure up. You see, I'm not actually short, but Naomi was (imperceptibly) taller than me. She never flaunted this, and was even a little self-conscious of it when I first met her. It seems a petty thing, to be so fixated on height, but still, I have never felt like a short man in my whole life, until I had met and fallen for her, and experienced what it feels like to be so small as to be beyond notice.

I sigh, this is getting depressing, and I have not come to Japan to feel sorry for myself, have I? I'm here to see two incredible people, my best friend, and the girl who I could not stop thinking about for the last few years. A Chinese proverb states that loving someone gives you courage, while being loved gives you strength. Or is it reversed? It doesn't matter, I tried to draw upon them both for courage and strength, shaking me out of my negative funk. It is time to lose myself in music, flashing lights, and the emotions of people in various states of inebriation: It is time to go clubbing.

The place I find isn't far from Dotonbori, but then again, most of the clubs are within walking distance of each other in this district. It seems to have a reputation for welcoming foreigners. One reviewer even recommended this place as a spot where locals and internationals came to mingle, so my lack of Japanese will not be a problem, I hope. It does cost several thousand Yen, but I discover that the ticket includes an all-you-can-drink entitlement. I like the idea of value, I hope they had lots of soda. However, it soon became clear to me that this might backfire, as after 20 minutes inside, there are quite a few people already pretty drunk. I see a lot of petting and groping, though no one had reacted badly, and some of the girls seemed to take it as a compliment. Then something caught my interest, a clear display of disinterest from a petite Asian girl, and some western guy.

"Hey, come on beautiful! I just wanna know your name!" This guy is starting to get pretty wasted. I don't want to sound too profiling, but with his frosted blond tips and heavy accent, he seems like your garden variety Euro-trash.

The girl he is trying to chat up is also trying to ignore him, but he's too drunk, stubborn, or stupid to get the message. Maybe even all three. This girl shows no sign of intimidation, answering him in a polite but icy manner. The music is playing quite a loud track right now, so I could only guess what she is saying because of the unwanted admirer.

"If you have a boyfriend, where is he? I know! How about I keep you company until he gets here! A fine girl like yourself is too pretty to be left alone!" He then attempts to put his arm around her, but she bats him away. I see a stunned look in his eyes that turns sullen and then dangerous as he slyly leers.

"Oh feisty, I like that! My turn!" She flinches as he looms over her and I see his hands lower behind her, a clear attempt to frisk her. It is now or never, Thomas Kei.

"Baby, there you are!" my voice booms cheerfully, catching both of their attention. I reach around the girl, initiating a hug, but keeping my arms, and hands, well on the outside of her body, spinning around and pulling her away from this guy before I enter the gap created. My back is to him, so he can't see the small smile and wink I give to reassure her that I was only trying to help. I then turn around, and give him a direct look. I'm not much taller than him, but he is much scrawnier, and probably only had light, superficial muscles under the shirt, a rich boy with glamour abs. I turn to face him with an even look and clench my mouth and inhale deeply, puffing out my chest. He gets the message. I glance and tilt my head to the left, and he notices security eyeing him with keen interest. This fight is over before it begins, and he isn't drunk enough to ignore their presence.

While he slinks away, I breathe a sigh of relief. Sure, I could have taken him, but foreigners shouldn't get into fights here, even if they don't start it. I face the girl, taking a good proper look at her. She is not tall, though not the shortest girl in the room, which isn't saying much as we are in Japan. A rosy complexion adds charm to her bright, warm chocolate eyes, delicately crafted cheekbones and dimples that enhance a pretty face. All underlined by an especially cute smile. Her hair is worn in an upright style, giving an almost regal frame to her innocent face, and her outfit's motif is "I'm a lady, so you'd better treat me as one!" She looks young, but I know she had to be at least 20 to be in a Japanese club. I lean forwards to speak without shouting.

"*Ojo-san daijoubu desuka?* (Are you alright miss?) She gave me a blank stare, then smiles apologetically, her eyes crinkling in a rather fetching manner.

She replies with, "Erm, sorry?"

I laugh, switching back to English.

"Are you okay?"

She quickly responds, "Oh yes! Sorry, I don't speak Japanese, only English!" She laughs, relieved when I smile and reply.

"Same, for the most part, but just in case you were a local, I wanted to get the message across. So you're okay?"

"Oh yeah, I'm fine, losers like him don't scare me, thanks again! Erm… just so you know, I do have a boyfriend… so, um," she seems hesitant to continue the line of conversation, almost as if she doesn't want to make things awkward for her knight in a long black coat. I'm touched, for she clearly has a kind heart, as well as a lot of experience with male attention. Conscientiousness is rarer with attractive people, and I know some very lovely faces masking disfigured, ugly hearts. I give a short laugh, again, and reassure her of my intentions.

"I heard, and I'm not surprised. It's okay, I'm not looking for anything like that. Though I must say, you are probably the cutest girl here. Your boyfriend is one lucky guy!" She seems visibly more comfortable now, not sensing any ulterior motives in my playful manner.

"He is, and I make sure he doesn't forget! He should have been here by now, but he lives in Kobe and messaged me earlier that there was a delay because of ice on the tracks. Apparently, the train conductor is apologising heaps. I'll introduce you once he gets here!"

"Cool! Would you like to get a drink? It is unlimited after all!"

"Hahah, I'm alright, but you go right ahead! Calvin loves beer, but I don't drink much." I assume Calvin is the boyfriend. We make our way to the bar counter, and I pick out a very colourful cocktail, which this girl finds amusing. We then make our way to a quieter section, away from the DJ, and I introduce myself.

"I'm Thomas, how do you do, young lady?"

"I'm Paris, and I am doing very well, thank you!" She giggles as I bow and sip the cocktail with my pinky finger held high, imitating high-class tea drinking.

"*Parlez vous Francais*, Paris (Do you speak French)?" I ask as a joke, but to my surprise she responds in pretty decent French. Much better than me anyhow.

"*Oui! Je parle un petit peu de Francais*!" Her smile widens as my brows arch up in surprise.

"*Tre bien! Magnifique*! I don't speak much French though, hahah!" She begins to relate to me how she had travelled across Europe, and that she found knowing some French to be very helpful in many of the countries. I question the origin of her name, and she mentions that her parents thought she would grow up to be beautiful and famous, like the city. I nod, to show my agreement.

"They weren't wrong! Hah! So are you on holiday here, like me?"

"Oh no, I work for a law firm here! I just started a couple of months ago, but sadly I haven't picked up much Japanese yet. It's crazy right?" She begins to tell me about the work hours and the commute, which together made for a mentally and physically draining schedule. Hearing about it makes me think of Naomi, and her own work schedule. She never said a word about the hours being such a toll, though I always assumed that she worked hard. I was touched, that she cared enough to not make me feel like a burden, despite coming to see her out of the blue. Like Vik and Maggy, although I suppose it was different for Team Panda.

"Oh, I have a friend here in Osaka, a lawyer too. I guess this place is really attractive to the profession! We're meeting tomorrow, in fact. Speaking of which, I read somewhere that Saturday is a working day for you people here?"

"Yeah, it is for a lot of people. That's why I came to the club tonight, I thought it might be quieter as Saturday night tends to be more popular. I'm a little disappointed by this place, but glad I met a new friend!"

"Really, where? Could you introduce me?" I pretend to scout around, looking high and low in an exaggerated manner. She laughs and playfully slaps my shoulder. I feel nothing but pretend to have suffered a devastating blow.

"Oh you! Hey, are you staying here much longer? My boyfriend doesn't like clubbing, he likes beers though. Why don't we go to a bar instead? I know this great one that does fried chicken!"

"What, karaage? I'm in!" She looks delighted that I want to join her. To be honest I had been at this place for about 40 minutes, and while it was alright, I wasn't much of a clubber or a drinker. I heard that this place was a popular spot for tourists and more accustomed to non-Japanese patrons. It probably is a good place for hook-ups, considering all the flirtatious overtures I pretend to not see in the shadows. Paris messages Calvin, who is outside, having just arrived, and is happy he doesn't need to pay the relatively high entrance fee (again though, depending on alcohol consumption, it could be one of the better value clubs). We make our way out, pausing to collect our jackets at the service desk. He is pretty easy to spot, being non-Asian, maybe Latino? If her boyfriend is surprised to see me, he hides it well, and his overall manner is one of calm, collected and easy going. I decide to diffuse any territorial instincts that might be lurking underneath the surface.

"This is Calvin? I'm very impressed, Paris, you didn't say he was so handsome! Pleased to meet you buddy, I'm Thomas." I give a firm handshake, which I pleasantly note he reciprocates. Paris is amused at the situation as Calvin's coolness is disarmed, and he warms up to me. She tells him about the unwanted attention back at the club, and holds her close, for his comfort as well as hers.

"But luckily Thomas was passing by and sensed my distress signal! I'm glad to have met him tonight."

"Likewise! I'm glad you were around, Thomas, that club is sort of known for sexually aggressive locals and foreigners, so I was getting anxious when Paris told me she was alone inside, and then I was stuck on a train! Not that it happens much here, it's surprisingly rare even in winter, that's how efficient this country is." I listen to his accent: American, West Coast, maybe even Los Angeles territory? The Latino background makes sense, I have a pen pal from California who is half-Japanese and half-Peruvian, speaks English, Japanese and Spanish. She jokingly referred to herself as Chifa, which is a term normally reserved for food (a fusion of Asian/Latin American). She had a normal Western name, but always referred to herself as Aoi Aoi-chan (literally Miss Blue-Blue), which I used whenever we corresponded. Despite a clash in our schedules (she was a nursing student who I guess is now a nurse) we had managed to Skype a few times, and Calvin's accent reminds me a lot of hers. Paris then expresses her shock about the club's reputation, because a co-worker had told her that it as a decent club for foreigners without Japanese fluency. Calvin elaborates.

"For guys it is, considering hooking up is pretty much what they want to do. A lot of the local girls I know tend to avoid it, unless they're feeling adventurous."

I learn that he is an English teacher here, and had come to Japan roughly the same amount of time ago that Paris did. Unlike her, he has a good grasp of Japanese, which is funny as we find the bar that Paris had mentioned earlier, and upon entering the staff instinctively look for Paris or me for orders. Calvin clearly expresses our desire for some drinks and lots of fried chicken, which speeds up the ordering process. Two beer pints, one orange for him and one green for me, arrive with a glass of lemon tonic water. We toast each other, glasses chinking as I had often seen in shows.

"Kanpai!" Calvin drains almost half of the glass, but I sip on my matcha beer (an infusion using green tea powder), enjoying the froth, which is not too bitter compared to most beers. The karaage arrives, three small platters filled with hot, crunchy lumps of fried chicken. I can tell Paris enjoys them immensely, as she finishes one platter and moves on to the next while Calvin and I share the third. We have a discussion about life experiences, especially how the two of them met. I had initially pegged Calvin at around 26, while Paris, I was assuming to be 22, only because she worked as a lawyer and thus needed to have spent at least four years on a degree. She is 23, so no surprises there, but to my astonishment her boyfriend reveals himself to be 33! He definitely has a mature vibe, but the features are dark and handsome, and did not have the tell-tale signs of someone in their 30s. For instance, his hair is thicker than mine, though I must admit I have naturally fine hair. I suppose if he had not shaved, I could believe around 28-30, but that clean trimmed face is another credit to his apparent vitality. I try to tactfully broach the subject with him, which he takes in good grace.

"If you asked me months ago what I thought of dating someone 10 years younger, I would probably have said that I wouldn't. But I also think that age is less about a number, and more about life experiences. For instance, if I had a full-time job, but dated someone starting college, that's a whole life experience apart. But after someone graduates and works, there's not a huge deal of contrast between their lifestyle and the lifestyle of someone in their 30s, or even 40s. I would probably still be working until my 50s, thanks to a horrible retirement package. Of course, starting your 60s is the milestone for another life adventure; that's going to be pretty wide divide if you are dating someone who just entered the work force!" We all nod at the practicality involved, and I think about the 'half age plus seven rule' that guys use to determine if a girl is too young. It works in this case anyway, and the two seem happy. Seeing the two of them, and how they interact, I could start to understand why a lot of girls prefer an older man as opposed to a young one, there is just so much more growth involved, for both parties. They ask me what I do and why I'm visiting Japan.

"I guess you could say I'm on an adventure, but I work as a subcontractor doing all types of things. I'd love to get into more detail, but I don't want to incriminate myself, there's a lawyer here after all." I wink at Paris, who indulges me,

"If you get me more karaage, I would consider you my client, and then I wouldn't be able to incriminate you!" We laugh at the entire concept, though we do order more karaage, along with French fries (for me), and Calvin orders his 3ʳᵈ beer. Paris wasn't kidding when she said the fried chicken was good. She picks up a piece with her chopsticks, about to bite into it, and then puts it down thoughtfully, as if she has realised something. Looking at me with a questioning gaze, she asks,

"Thomas, I'm sorry if this is a little personal, but you're not gay are you?"

I smile, this isn't the first time I'm asked after all. I playfully wink at Calvin, who is amused by my antics. "No," I reply, clearly humoured by this.

"Do you have a girlfriend?"

I laugh, another question I've heard before. I shake my head, and she continues,

"But that friend you're seeing tomorrow, is it a girl?"

I'm intrigued, this isn't in my usual list of commonly asked questions, but I can't fault the inquisitive lawyer mind frame on display. Realising she may have been rude, she turns wide-eyed and pink-cheeked, which I find adorable, and starts to apologise. I laugh to show her I am not offended.

"Actually, to be honest, it is a girl I'm seeing tomorrow. I have been into someone, for a while now. I'm in love with her, actually. It's part of the reason I'm in Japan, I'm trying to figure out how I feel once I see her again."

"That sounds so romantic! Is she a nice person?" Paris is openly interested, though I suppose romance is something a lot of women express a natural affinity in hearing about.

"She's probably one of the best people I know. Smart, driven, funny, gorgeous, and very kind, but enough about me, she's pretty cool too!" She smiles, and the earlier tension is noticeably diffused. I continue,

"Maybe I was in that club because I wanted to stop thinking so much. I really wasn't there for a hook up. I swear! I just like to absorb the vibe at such scenes, it's kind of… calming, do you know what I mean?" She nods while musing over my words, maintaining eye contact.

"Sorta, yeah! After a long day I just want to unwind and live in the moment. Um, do you have a photo of her? Could I, maybe, see what she looks like?"

"Sure, let me bring one up on Facebook. I don't really keep photos on my phone." I laugh, but I also begin to feel a sense of trepidation, which I dismiss as nerves. I brush it aside from my mind, and I find a decent photo of the two of us. "Here she is, didn't I tell you she was beautiful?"

Paris watches keenly as I show her Naomi, then I see her brown eyes widen in shock, like fawn, and a small gasp slips from her now covered mouth. Clearly, the picture was better than I thought, and Paris is obviously in awe. So why is my heart thudding so loudly!? Paris says something in an audible whisper. I feel a rush to my head, pupils dilating, as she looks directly at me again.

"That's – is her name Naomi? I work with her!"

Chapter 16

I am aware that my breathing has quickened, but I do my best to appear calm. Hopefully, I hide my shock, as she is open with hers. Swallowing, I answer,

"You know Naomi? And you work with her? That's great!" I keenly focus my gaze on her, reiterating what she has just revealed. Paris nods repeatedly, and then continues to explain.

"Well, I don't work WITH her, she's much more senior than me. But I see her around the office. Always calm and focused, I really feel motivated working at the same firm. Oh um, one time we were having drinks at an office party and I spoke to her too, she's really nice, really chill."

"She's always been like that, I wasn't exaggerating before!" I laugh as a sign of relief, which Paris joins in. I sense that we are both slightly reeling from this revelation. Maybe this is a divine sign, meeting her may have been no accident after all. Paris doesn't know much about Naomi's personal life, but she is able to give me an impression of the woman she had become. She grows hesitant about saying something, which turns out to be about Naomi's current relationship status.

"Erm, I thought she was dating someone… I don't know who, but won't that make it difficult for you if you're still in love with her?" She looks puzzled when I smile gently and respond,

"It doesn't matter who she's dating, as long as they're treating her well. She's smart, so I think she did figure out I liked her, but I'm not sure if she knows that I loved her, that I'm still in love with her. I wanted to tell her because this might be the last chance I get before my life changes forever."

"Oh no, are you dying?!" Paris is so sweet, no wonder she still looks so young – her innocence was keeping age at bay. I don't think she was naïve either, just not embittered by the world.

"Oh goodness no! I'm quite healthy, and just between us, I think I may likely be immortal! But my circumstances have changed, and soon I may not be in a position to tell her what I've been keeping in all these years, either because of my family duty or my spiritual detachments." I explain to them about my parents and the conversation which triggered all of this, even mentioning parts of the conversation I held with Vik. Calvin says something at last,

"That's really heavy to lay on you man. But, you act like getting married or removing yourself from society are the only two options. Isn't there anything else you want to pursue?"

"There might be, but to be honest, I think that subconsciously maybe my friend was right, maybe I am not moving forward with my life because I haven't dealt with what I'm feeling. Like ghosts who can't move on, maybe people like me are bound by unresolved feelings. In that case, coming here and making my peace with everything might be the best course of action. The truth is, I don't know what to do, but I'm hoping that when I return I'll have some clue."

"Hey, you're a poet, and you didn't even know it!" Paris lightens the mood with wordplay. I couldn't help but join in.

"I like to rhyme, all the time!" We look at Calvin, who simply grins and states,

"Oranges. Purple." I take the bait, and reply with,

"Lozenges, Whirlpool!" We laugh as he raises his brows in surprise, and nods approvingly. It is technically not a true rhyme, but we are having silly fun so it doesn't matter. All talk of Naomi gives way, as we simply discuss whatever comes to mind, though it might be that they wished to avoid the topic, to spare me any discomfort. We have a good time for another hour, and at that point decide to take our leave. I cover the bill, which the two are slightly taken aback by. They insist on paying, I insist on paying, and in the end I accept their coins as repayment: they are more interesting than notes, and I'm gathering as much as I can to take back home, having donated most of my previous collection to Inari. We head outside and make our way to the subway.

They are heading to the JR, then to a place called Konoikeshinden: Paris lived around there. I recall that Calvin lived in Kobe, but it is a Friday night, so he might be staying with her, or simply going home after he had walked her back safely. We part ways there, swapping Facebook details to ensure we could keep in touch. I could have taken a subway directly to my area, Tanimachiyonchome, but it is barely a 30-minute walk and I have some restless energy to disperse before I go back home. I take my time in getting back, not caring when I get back. I feel quite safe here, my mood pensive, and the cold is no bother.

Tonight I had met someone who works with Naomi, and unwittingly I confessed how I felt to them. Will she be angry with me, if she came to know? Or will she also find it a bizarre coincidence, and we will laugh about it like old times. Expressing my feelings was very cathartic, in the past 6 days I had spoken more about my unrequited feelings than in the past six years, and getting it off my chest is already giving me greater perspective. By the time I make it back, I feel my mind clearing from the walk. Naomi is my friend, and regardless of what happens tomorrow I wouldn't dishonour that fact. She's been a great friend, but I do think that most of that is due to her being a great person, and not because we have anything special. That connection belongs to my xiong di Vik. I think the Japanese term for that is 'nakama', or 'aibo', although 'aibo' might be closer to 'partners in crime'. But in regards to Naomi, maybe deep down I am putting too much pressure on what friendship means. Maybe I'm actually a terrible friend, because I wasn't able to trust her with how I felt… She had usually been sincere with me, yet even now, six years later, I'm acting like some pretentious fool. Okay! I've decided, tomorrow I will tell her the truth, but I will also not allow it to jeopardise our relationship… Damn it! I realise, for the umpteenth time, that I need to rethink this, but in the morning, when I've slept on it.

Returning to my hotel, I shower as soon as I get the hot water working; I set the temperature for 60 degrees Celsius and crouch in the tub, letting the hot water wash over me. It soon fills the tub; I always plug up a bathtub if I intend to keep the water on for more than three minutes; sometimes I feel the urge to sit in a tub as I contemplate my thoughts. Psychologists might attribute it to an urge to recreate the womb environment, the urge to feel safe and protected. They would be right. I need to sleep, mentally there is a lot to process from today, and I'm driving myself crazy trying to think of what to do. As Alan Watts used to say, "To understand chaos, one must surrender themselves to the dance," and I simply let go, as I drift away into unconsciousness.

Chapter 17

I awaken at around 6 am, climb out of the bathtub, then go back to sleep, this time in my bed. I reawaken, and discover that it is 10:14 am. I should get up, check out is due at 11 am. Today is it. Strangely enough, I awoke with a calm and clarity of mind and heart. It wasn't that I had any answers, I was simply unintimidated by what uncertainties lay ahead. I moisturise my face, do my best to clean the black coat and scarf I have been wearing since I got to this country, and take out the present I have been carrying in my now spacious luggage case. With it in one hand, and the luggage case in the other, I make my way downstairs to the reception, and leave the hotel within five minutes. The weather is pretty sunny, but I'm glad that it is still cold; I don't want my gift to melt, not after all this time, after all of the distance travelled. As I wait at the station to reach Umeda, I catch my reflection. The man I see looks a little grim, and I remind myself that today is happy one, and at the very least I can try to enjoy it. Taking a deep breath, mirror me looks a little less sombre, with less restrictive body language.

I arrive at Umeda Station at about 12:30 pm, and decide to explore the area a little. It is a business district, plenty of shops and boutiques too, but everything is inside the skyscrapers and other complexes that lined the streets. Once it becomes 12:50 pm, I use my phone to look for the 7/11, walking to the underground convenience store. I wait, until 1:10 pm, when I get her message.

Naomi: Heyy! I'm here! Where are you?

Thomas: I'm here at the 7/11, Umeda right?

Naomi: Yep. I don't see you?

Thomas: I don't see you? Lol. I'll walk around.

After I circle the place, I realise something so stupid that I could have kicked myself.

Thomas: Hey, guess who's an idiot?

Naomi: You.

            Hahahah!

            Why tho??

Thomas: The subway 7/11 is not the JR 7/11

Naomi: Lol, do you want to meet at Yodobashi instead?

Thomas: Hahah, yeah, I can see it, race you there!

I head into a big building, with 'YODOBASHI' in big letters at the front. 8th floor, dining level. Meet by the elevators. I press buttons, impatient to get there. I curse inwardly. This is not a good start! Finally, one becomes available, I anxiously get in, punch in the number 8, and the elevator takes a painfully slow pace to get to level 8. I step off, and I'm pleased to see she hasn't reached here yet. I steady my nerves, quickly give myself a pat down to groom myself, and I wait. After a few minutes, I take out my phone, and send her a message.

Thomas: Hey, I think I win.

Naomi: Huh? Why?

Thomas: I made it before you?

Naomi: Lvl 8, Yodobashi, by the elevators?

Thomas: Lvl 8, Yodobashi, by the elevators. Lol.

I scan around, and I determine that there are a separate set of elevators on this floor. Makes sense, this place is huge after all. Still, this is **not** the impression I wanted to make! I glance around, and then I see her. The Buddha mentions that when you find your soul mate, your heart will not beat faster and you will not become flustered. Instead, you will feel calm in a way that you've never previously experienced.

I'm not sure how it was possible but as she walks towards me, time seems to slow down in a way I haven't experienced in over six years. My mind takes a flashback to the first time I saw her, but this wasn't the girl in the yellow top, denim skirt and sandals: I'm being greeted by a young woman who walks in an elegantly confident stride. The light grey long coat she's wearing matches the blue-grey pants, and her skin, oh I had forgotten until now, is more brilliant than the full moon. Underneath the coat, she has a slim fitting dark sweater, which only serves to highlight her flowing black hair, cascading past her lovely face. A burgundy scarf complements her bright red lips, which are smiling at me as her hands wave back and forth in a most welcoming manner. Yet amidst all this, it's her eyes that I'm most drawn to, the same beautiful eyes which I had looked into all those years ago, and found that they housed an achingly beautiful soul. It is impossible for me to not smile in elation as she approaches. She radiates strength, self-confidence, and yet, also the same down-to-earth attitude from before.

"Hey, Tom!" Even her voice, still that of a fun-loving girl, has taken a slightly huskier undertone. It is all incredibly alluring.

"Hi, Naomi." My voice is subdued, I take a moment to gather myself. I flash a grin, and try to act like 'me'. "It really has been too long!"

"I know right!" We hug briefly, before exploring the dining options available to us. I didn't care where we ate, I just insist she takes us anywhere with food she enjoyed. There is so much I wanted to say, to share with her, to hear about her, but I'm in no rush – my feelings had waited almost seven years, they can wait a little longer. She casually selects a place that does rice dishes, and we're seated in a booth by the window. We remove our scarves, and she her jacket, but I keep mine on.

"I still can't believe it, you're actually here!" She looks at me intensely for a moment. I force myself out of my daze.

"I can't believe it either! You've become a beautiful woman." She laughs, before responding,

"You look different, I've never seen you with glasses and short hair before." I suppose it's true, I had never worn my glasses around Naomi if I could help it, though I didn't actually need them before unless I wanted to see long distance at night. Even now, I only wear them because I'm in Japan, and want to have uncompromised visuals of my surroundings. As for my hair, I had cut it before I came here, before I left for Japan. I was going for a look that suggested I was more mature now. It was my turn again,

"Your voice, it's so professional and confident. This place must agree with you!" She nods, before commenting on how I sound.

"You sound a little different too. Calmer. Less…"

"Less weird?"

"A little, but more like you don't have four or five things you want to say at once. It's nice." I smile, for there's so much I want to say, but somehow I don't need to think about it with her, it just happens. The waitress arrives, and Naomi orders a seafood rice set, while I order an eel rice set. And a serve of French fries of course. While we wait for our meals, Naomi prepares some tea: she tears open a packet of green tea powder for each of us, and pours hot water into our cups. I thank her, and we toast each other. She explains that this place serves a rice dish that involves mixing the tea with the rice. I recall it from my sukiyaki experience in Kyoto, and she is slightly impressed when I reveal that I know of it.

"Oh wow, you know about it?" I relate my time in Kyoto. The meal, anyway.

"Yes, but I've only had ochazuke the one time, so I'll just copy you."

"The instructions are better." She points them out, the instructions that are located in the menu stand, available in English. I look over briefly, but I'm not too interested, not with Naomi sitting in front of me. Sitting here, I'm staring at her; I can't help it! It all seems surreal. She notices me as she glances over from the menu. Remembering that I do have something to give her, I take the white gift bag I have carried in my luggage since I began this trip. Today, however, it will at last see the light of day. I prepare myself as I take it out from under the table.

"My dearest Naomi, please accept this as a token for all the missed birthdays and holidays over the years! It has made its way across the seas, from Tokyo to Mt Fuji, up Fushimi Inari in Kyoto, and finally found its way to you in Osaka. I hope you like it." She seems amused at my proclamations, and thanks me as she accepts the laminated bag.

"Aww, thank you, you really didn't have to!" She looks inside, and curiously examines the contents. I had searched for chocolates and sweet treats from home, things which would be rarer to find in Japan, and I was fortunate the weather was chilled enough as to keep them preserved (though I had been careful with my luggage case for that reason). Previously, I had considered all manner of luxurious gifts for her, until I realised that she could have gotten such things herself if she really wanted them. The thoughtful angle was the way to go, but over the years I wasn't sure what she was still into, so aside from various sweets I settled for something sweeter: nostalgia. She examines the empty jar of Nutella, with a custom label that spelled her name 'Naomi', and a small towel that featured a little anime character she enjoyed (a blue Totoro).

Over the years I had gifted her with various Totoro-themed merchandise, partially as a joke, and partially because she adored them. When she graduated and left for Japan, I grew ambitious, deciding that I would make her something unique. I bought materials and spent a few weeks slowly hand sewing a medium-sized plush toy, until I was able to craft a pretty decent grey Totoro. It was tailored for her, as I had added a graduation cap (also self-made) that included a small blessing if she were to ever remove the fabric from the mortarboard, and dressed in a set of graduation robes. I found this part trickier, as I had cut the edge in a jagged fashion to represent a ghostly feature; an in-joke from a fan theory that suggested Totoro was actually the grim reaper, and the girls from that iconic movie had died at the start of the film. But I included it to represent the idea of moving on, for the toy to symbolise a guardian spirit (of sorts) while she made a new life elsewhere. Did it sound like a deep concept? It looked disappointingly tacky compared to the rest of the plushy, but at that point I had run out of time, so decided to stick with it instead of making another one. I was skipping for days when she told me she liked it. On this occasion, I was once again pressed for time, and could not exercise my creative side.

Our food arrives, and I have to say that they are served in an exquisite bamboo steamer, with the main toppings resting on white rice. A dainty little pot for the ochazuke comes with the meal, which includes an assortment of pickled side vegetables. My French fries arrive on a boat styled platter, but I leave them for now. We eat and talk, between bites, of the old days, and I fill her in on as much information as I can. I tell her about the people we knew, the couples still together, and the ones who are now married with kids. I tell her that Toby is now involved in a lot of local theatre, and Louise is currently working in a lab while trying to find an ideal housemate.

"You know, they both asked me to sneak you back with me in my luggage, but I think that as a lawyer you could afford something slightly fancier." She laughs, it sounds like the peal of bells. Then she relates her work life, which is as busy as I had heard from Paris. I ask her about her non-work life. When she mentions dating, I am surprised to find that I don't feel any stabs of pain in my chest, no jealousy or envy: I just wanted to know if they were good to her.

"When I'm not travelling, it's actually pretty boring. I work, and I sometimes hang out with the office crew, but I don't have any friends here like our old group. I try dating, with apps, and I meet a few guys, but there's no one serious. I mean, there's this one guy, right now, he's a dental student so his hours are clashing with my work schedule. Plus he's not replying to my messages, so I don't really know what we are. How about you? Have you found someone?"

This is a tricky question for me to answer, but I decide to wait before telling Naomi why I had come to Japan. It isn't being dishonest, I decide, I will reveal the truth soon.

"Oh, nothing serious, I tried dating apps too, but no one really clicks with me. Actually, that's kind of why I came to Japan – it's my birthday soon."

"Oh yeah, happy birthday! I'll probably forget, so this is an early one just in case!"

"Thank you! You've always been so considerate of me. Yeah, I'm turning 29 in a few days, so I wanted to go somewhere different, look back on the last 10 years before I'm 30."

"I think that's great. I travelled to a lot of places, when I can, and I really like experiencing new things. It's part of the reason I came to Japan, I wanted a life that wouldn't become a routine. I think that if I hadn't, I might have gotten married, maybe even have kids by now… but I don't know if I want that yet, I just really enjoy my life, you know?"

"I do, my parents are urging me to marry, they say I'm getting old. Can you believe that?" I wink, to suggest that I do actually think I am getting old.

"My parents are the same, they want me to settle down and give them grandkids! It's lucky you picked now to come see me, if you came next week I would be busy seeing them and we wouldn't get to hang out." She and I look at each other, it was now or never, and I take a leap of faith.

"I still like you." The words come out, however, I back out last second, by smiling playfully, which robs the words of their impact, so Naomi thinks I am just joking round.

"You're very sweet, Tom. I'm glad you came to see me too." She smiles, and I continue mine, though I feel massive disappointment. I look away, and Naomi seems to notice that I want to say something. My tone changes to something more serious when I ask her,

"Haven't you ever wanted to get married, once you fall in love with the right person?" She looks thoughtful and thinks for a moment before telling me,

"I've never fallen in love before. I wouldn't know what I want if it happened. But I know that I love being me right now, so I guess it's just a matter of when it happens."

Something incredible is happening to me; I thought I was in love with Naomi, but the more we talk, the more it feels like I'm falling in love with her all over again. Yet stranger still, I no longer feel like confessing my feelings for her. The way she is now, the way she was when living life to the fullest, she is perfect. That is the person I loved. Telling her how I felt all this time simply isn't what she needs to hear. We make more small talk, drink more tea, and then I suggest we leave. There is some shopping she wants to do, on the 2nd floor of this multi-storey building that seems to have everything a consumer could want to buy. She looks at my fries, which I haven't touched, and confirms if I'm truly finished. I act as cheerfully as I can.

"Yes, I'm done. I don't need those fries. Let's go."

We are presented with the bill, which I insist on covering. It is my last day in Japan, and I don't need yen after this, so she relented. We take the elevator to the second floor, and she finds what she needs pretty quickly: a new type of film that produced Polaroid photos by imprinting smart phone images. It's easy to use, all you need to do is to place it over the screen and voila, instant picture (within 20 seconds or so). We take a picture together outside the elevator, while we wait for one to make its way up, and I am amazed that we look so photogenic. Well, she always looked that good, but I like the way I look in that photo, despite my face being a little flushed (something that had nothing to do with the coat I had kept on during the meal). As we travel to the ground floor, she asks me what I want to do now. She seems surprised that I'm leaving this evening, as she has been prepared to hang out for the entire Saturday. It's tempting, but I don't really have a reason to be here anymore, and I want her to have more time in clearing out her office space before seeing her family. At the same place Paris worked. A curiosity sparks within, and I make a request.

"Oh, you work around this area right? Can I see your office building before I go?"

"Sure, but you aren't allowed inside without a security pass, sorry!"

"It's okay, I just wanna see where you work, where the magic happens!"

"Hahah, you're still so weird!"

"I guess I am, hahah!"

As we make our way to her office, I take note of the surroundings. I suddenly decide I'm not satisfied with leaving things as they are. I talk to her as we walk through the crowds, their presence helping to mask my anxieties.

"Hey, Naomi, do you wanna play a quick game? It's called 'What If?'." We've made it to the office, or at least, the building that houses the office. Naomi indulges me, though I can see she is a little puzzled.

"What if, I might be getting married soon?" She gasps, and reprimands me for not telling her sooner.

"Really?? That's something you should say at the start of a conversation!"

"Well, I said, 'might be'! I'm not sure if I want to do that, or join a priesthood somewhere instead."

"Oh really? You should definitely consider marriage! Right?" She seems more intrigued now, and I steady myself.

"That's what the game is for. You see, what if – what if I came to Japan to see the last girl I had feelings for, so I could make sense of how I feel now?" She is looking more confused now, but figures it out. I can't look at her directly, but try to keep a poker face. Her beautiful eyes widen, and are looking directly at me when she says,

"Me? But that was so long ago! Wasn't it?" I look at her directly, taking off my frames so she could see the truth in my eyes.

"What if I'm still in love with her? I don't mind if she doesn't feel the same. But if she asked, I would go anywhere in the world to see her. I know she doesn't want that, so it makes me not want it either. I don't think we only became friends out of me wanting something more, but I want her to know that I don't regret it, that she was worth it." I put on a smile. It's not a far cry from my true feelings, which are turbulent, but also strangely happy that I have said it, at last. Naomi looks at me with a mixture of understanding and sadness as she tells me, gently, kindly,

"Well, Tom, I hope you found what you were looking for."

"I think I did, thank you for everything. I should go now."

"It was really great seeing you again, Thomas!" I don't trust my voice, but I nod to show her my sentiments were the same. We embrace, and I maintain the hold for a second longer than she does.

"Bye!"

"Bye." I watch as she enters those glass doors, walking out of sight and out of my life once more.

The whole experience has left me woozy, and I slowly make my way outside, where I find myself on a bridge overlooking the city. My breathing is irregular and heavy. I lean on the rails for support, doing my best to maintain balance and composure. I am then hit by a sight I will likely never forget, due to the association with this memory. A bright beam of light is emanating from the sunset, which shone gold for a moment, before taking on an orange hue. My strength returns as I try to make sense of what I am feeling.

Naomi's blossomed into the woman I glimpsed inside her, all those years ago. I came here because I was in love with the girl, and I wanted to tell her that before moving on. Instead, I fell in love with the woman, and in doing so, I get a sense of how much I've grown in the last six years. Love makes fools of us all. Yet a fool who persists in his folly becomes wise, so sayeth William Blake. If I am that fool, then I wonder who is laughing at me? Maybe I should just laugh at myself, for everything that led me here in the first place was what I am confronting again, at the end of my trip.

I make my way to the Umeda train station, and take the connections that will take me to Kansai Airport. The image of the setting sun is still on my mind, and I look at my reflection in the compartment windows. What I see is a strangely subdued man, eyes sombre but no longer as desperate for a voice. I'm glad that the atmosphere in Japan favoured peace and quiet, I want tranquillity as I process how I feel.

Calvin, from the previous night, had sent a message warning me of how certain train compartments went to the airport, while the others continued travelling along the countryside. It's not a mistake I will want to make if I need to be punctual. It does put me in a state of paranoid alertness, but fortunately the entire train goes to the airport, and from there, it's simply a matter of procedure and waiting times.

Home. I will be home soon, but my brief time in Japan makes me rethink the implications of such a word. Is it a place that I'm familiar with, a structure of routine, or can it be that home is where I feel the most welcome? Vik and Maggy took me into their home and made me feel welcomed, but while he and I shared a powerful camaraderie, I wasn't truly at home with just his presence. For that matter, I wouldn't call what I felt with Naomi being 'at home' either. No, what I need is something that was predominantly me, but as to what that was, I still have no clue.

My brain is swimming in a neural cocktail, simultaneously sobering my mind and filling my soul with a restless energy. Tomorrow evening I will be back home. Oscar will be waiting for me at the airport, he will take me back to my house, and maybe in-between we will be eating late night fast food… it is hard to imagine that I have only been in Japan for about a week. What will become of Jake and Soo-Jung? It's his first real relationship, but no matter what becomes of it, he'll definitely grow from the experience. Had I been able to do so while I was here?

Now that I am just waiting for my departure flight: it seems as if I'm going back as a different person. They do say travelling broadens the mind, enriches the soul, and puts one's life into perspective. While I have gained a measure of the latter, I still don't know if I want to become a celibate priest, or start a family, or maybe neither?

What I can say is that my heart has opened, after remaining closed for so long. I felt, and still feel, a rush of emotions I've been suppressing, as well as feelings I've since forgotten. I am alive with sensations and the experience is testament of my choice to truly live. Maybe I'm too young to be a sage, to give up everything, and especially to cease feeling the feelings which are part of the journey to enlightenment. I think about Naomi again. I didn't have to place my life on hold, but I don't have to throw away a timeless connection either, do I? Maybe in this life it isn't meant to be, and maybe I have just arrived at these feelings too early. My soul can wait, whether it is a few years, a decade, even the next life, until the time we will be able to comprehend each other.

In the meantime, life is too short to stay closed off from the world. Off to the next adventure!

I want to explore more connections, those threads that link us to the world where we learn to live and love, laugh and eventually let go. But before that, I want to transcribe my feelings, which culminated in the image of that sunset vivid in my mind.

The Osaka Sunset

What assurances doth Life provide?
Carpe Diem, quam minimum, credula postero.

In the land of the Rising Sun,
I see Osaka's sun, setting.
In twilight, I fight regrets of which I struggle in forgetting.
Neither Day nor Night,
I seek insights, before Darkness envelops my lonely heart.

Breathe… a gentle breeze reminds me to Breathe…

Long ago there lived a people who loved the Sun, too.
Yet love became obsession, their humanity regressed,
'Til but macabre yearnings for light was left.
Great beauty, sullied by those prisoners of love who offered
their very lives,
Sun worshippers, in love with the idea of Light.

I seek to understand True Love
Which cannot be captured, only shared.
All fears and controlling desire,
Pale against that Heavenly Fire.

From where did it come? A quiet mystery.
Maybe it was always here?
Passing each day, never to stay,
and returning somewhere each night.
Her warmth my privilege, not my right.

What does it mean to hope and dream,
when you must relinquish,
One's very illumination?
It is as simple as breathing.
The air is all around us.
Respiration.
Fill your lungs, then empty...
Resist the folly of keeping it in,
What gives joyous life grows stale in your prison.

In the land of the Rising Sun
Twilight fades and makes way for Night.
I can let go of the light, but I'll never forget,
How Beautiful and Bright, the Osaka Sunset.

Epilogue

I barely remember getting home, content with reliving my memories, until I'm snapped out of my thoughts by Oscar. It's almost 1 am. My friend has been waiting for longer than I have intended owing to a mistake made with the check-in times, as well an issue that arose with the quarantine officers (not with me personally, some other people on holiday). I was almost vetted on a 'random basis', but once it was known that I was a local returning home, the whole process became relaxed, casual, and much quicker.

"Oscar! Sorry for the wait man, I thought I told you when I stopped over in Singapore, come an hour later and avoid the waiting times!" In typical fashion, he just shrugs stoically.

"Eh, I don't mind. Had nothing better to do."

I insist we get out of the airport and offer to pay for those exorbitant parking fees we're charged. We do end up stopping at a McDonald's, and although he asks me about the trip, I am not really in the mood to go into detail. He doesn't ask me about Naomi, which I am grateful for because I have only just finished processing our last moments together, my physiological and mental states are almost back to normal, except I still feel as if I'm glowing somehow. We finish eating and he takes me home with few words exchanged – I suppose he's tired too, it being as late as it is. But I'm not really too tired to make conversation, I'm just preoccupied with planning. For the first time in a long time, I feel like I'm... unstuck? A feeling in-between motivated and inspired: rejuvenated. Yes, I haven't felt more recharged since I was a wide-eyed youngster, and this sensation is something my adult self recognised as powerful.

Reflecting on my life to this point, the choices made, as well as the directions it's heading, I must admit that Vik had a point about me not following my true ambitions.

We arrive at my house, and I decline Oscar's help in unpacking – I travelled light, and returned even lighter in every sense of the word. I wish him a safe journey home, and make my way inside a dusty interior, unpacking, showering, and then retiring to my bed. Ah, spacious sleeping space, the only thing lacking from the Japanese bedroom experience. Well, the only thing that didn't require another person anyway. Lying down, unwinding, I close my eyes, and think of what I will do now. I think to myself,

Well, Thomas, your birthday is coming up soon, an auspicious date to be reborn. Did you find yourself while overseas? Do you have an answer as to who you are meant to be?

I smile, at peace with my resolutions, before settling into my rest. Tomorrow's another day, another opportunity to raise my forgotten dreams from their slumber. I will greet each sunrise as my idealistic comrade, and each sunset a reminder of life's ephemeral beauty. Maybe, it is all one needs to make it through Life.